CYCLOPS AND PHOENIX

adapted by
Paul Mantell and Avery Hart

based on comics by Scott Lobdell

cover illustration by Steve Lightle

D1649098

Random House Sprinters
Random House 🏠 New York

Chapter 1

Jean Grey sat on the deserted beach, under the palm trees, watching them sway in the breeze. Her eyes swept the horizon from the north shore of the island of St. Bart's, one of the most radiant islands in the Caribbean. She looked out over the blue-green water toward the spot where her husband was windsurfing.

Her *husband*. She still couldn't get used to calling him that! After all, she and Scott Summers had only been married for three wonderful days. Of course, they'd been in love practically forever, ever since they'd first come to Professor Charles Xavier's School for Gifted Youngsters, so many years ago.

Gifted youngsters, indeed! What would the people of the world say if they knew that, in reality, the school had been the training ground for Professor Xavier's team of mutants—the X-Men!

Jean was half-tempted to psi-link telepathically with the X-Mansion, just to say hello to all their friends back home. But she decided against it. A honeymoon was a time to be alone together.

Over the years, there had hardly been a moment when they and their fellow X-Men weren't engaged in one life-and-death struggle or another. They had earned this vacation.

Scott waved to her, smiling, the sun glinting off his ruby quartz glasses. He dared not take the glasses off, even here. Without them, his optic blasts would obliterate whatever he looked at. It was why they all called him Cyclops—but to her, he would always be Scott.

Waving at her threw him off balance. Scott fell from his board and plunged headlong into the water. Jean laughed, clapping as he came sputtering to the surface. "Nice going, King of the Waves!" she called teasingly.

"That does it!" he shouted back. "I'm coming out, so get ready to be buried up to your pretty neck in the sand!"

She watched him emerging from the sea, the droplets of water shining on his bronzed body.

"Daydreaming again?" Scott teased as he

sat down beside her. He seemed to have forgotten all about his threat to bury her in the sand.

"Oh, I was just remembering the wedding," Jean said. "Wasn't it beautiful, Scott?"

"Amazing," he agreed, brushing a lock of her long, wavy red hair off her face and kissing her tenderly. "All those people, mutants and humans, together in one place, at one time..."

"I wonder if there'll ever be another day like it," Jean said, sighing.

Scott frowned. "Why shouldn't there be?"

"You know what I mean," she said. "There are so many threats and dangers. We've all been through so much sadness."

He gazed at her. Even through the ruby quartz glasses, she saw the pain in his eyes.

"Do you think we'll ever have a family together, Scott?" she whispered.

He looked down at the sand. "You're thinking of Nathan Christopher...and Rachel... aren't you?" he asked.

Jean did not answer. She winced as she thought of Rachel Summers, the daughter she and Scott had given birth to in an alternate time line. Jean had never really been a mother to Rachel. She'd never had the chance.

And then there was Nathan Christopher,

Scott's son by Jean's clone, Madelyne Pryor. Nate had been kidnapped by the X-Men's old enemy Apocalypse—who infected the baby with a life-threatening techno-virus.

Jean shook her head at her own stupidity. How could she have expected Scott to think about them having a family of their own, so soon after Nate's kidnapping?

"I'm sorry, Scott," she said sincerely. "I shouldn't have brought it up."

"No, that's all right," he told her, putting an arm around her shoulders. "Maybe someday—but Jean, how can we have a family, and still be X-Men? We'd be exposing our children to constant danger. We'd always be off somewhere, fighting evil, never together long enough to have a real family life—"

"That didn't stop you before," Jean reminded him.

"If only I'd known then what I know now," he said sadly.

"Don't say that, Scott," she urged. "Maybe it's all been for the best. The Askani woman who saved Nate from Apocalypse and took him into the future said Nathan had a great destiny. Maybe she was right. If he can save the people of her time, maybe it was worth all the pain you went through."

"Come on," he said, taking her hand. "Let's forget it. Let's go for a nice, long swim. After all, it's our honeymoon!"

At the water's edge, he took her in his arms and kissed her. When they finally broke apart, he gave her a playful shove and raced ahead of her into the water. "Last one in does the dishes forever!" he called back to her.

"Scott, you brat!" Jean laughed and dove in after him. She would follow him to the ends of the Earth. In fact, she already had.

But for now, for today, and for the next ten days, nothing would disturb their happiness. Nothing...noth—huh?!? What was that?

"Scott!" Jean screamed as she felt the first, powerful tug. It yanked at her suddenly, grabbing her by the back of the neck, lifting her clear out of the water.

Or *was* she out of the water? She couldn't even tell! She could see only bright, flashing, multi-colored light. Her ears filled with an unearthly roar she couldn't define.

"Scott!" she shrieked as the roar grew louder. She felt herself spinning upward, downward, inward, outward. "Scott, where are you? What's happening?"

Chapter 2

Bursts of color exploded all around her in brilliant red and orange, and the accompanying thunderclaps sounded like explosions.

No—they *were* explosions. Jean could see that now. Everything around her was in flames. Shells and missiles were landing every few seconds.

A moment ago, she could feel the delicious warmth of the tropical sun on her skin. She could smell the salt water that surrounded her on every side. Now, all she felt was the dry, searing heat of a roaring inferno.

A moment ago, she had closed her eyes in paradise…only to open them now in a nightmare.

But where was she? Jean's vision soon grew focused enough for her to see. And she found herself in the strangest place she had ever been. She was in restraints, strapped to a small platform. It was one of many that protruded from the upper stories of a towering, sky-scraper-like structure.

The deafening explosions wracked the surroundings, and platform after platform was blasted into oblivion. The people standing on them were hurled into the abyss below. A massacre was in progress—and she was going to be among the victims if she didn't get out of there in a hurry!

Instinctively, Jean struggled against her restraints, and soon managed to free herself. "Instinctively," because her entire life, it seemed, had been one long struggle.

In her youth, she had struggled to control her own blossoming psionic powers—the mutant abilities that took her years to learn how to handle.

As a woman, she and her friends had fought for years to protect a world that feared and hated them simply for what they were.

But not today. Today was the first day of her honeymoon.

"All right," she muttered aloud, standing up and stretching her aching muscles. "I'm not too proud to say it. I'm officially confused. One minute we're lounging on the shores of

St. Bart's, the next, I'm alone in the absolute middle of...of *what*?!"

She looked around at what was left of the bizarre structure. About twenty feet away from her was a man. He was unconscious and hanging by one arm from the edge of a platform. Only the restraints held him there, and they were badly frayed.

Jean quickly glanced around one more time. The blasts were still coming. Corpses littered all the other remaining platforms. A hundred feet to the left of her, a direct hit sent one platform plummeting earthward.

The structure itself seemed almost...almost human—certainly techno-organic, at least. But whoever had built it, whoever had inhabited it, was gone now. Dead or fled—except for the man hanging there below her.

She focused once more on the unconscious fellow. Seeing his face as he slowly twirled around, Jean realized he was no one she recognized. But he seemed human, at least. And he was certainly someone who could use a hand from her.

Springing into action, Jean reached out telekinetically to pull him to her—only to find that nothing happened!

Where had her mutant powers gone? She hadn't the slightest idea. But the man below her was in grave danger, and she wasn't about to let him die. Too many had died in this massacre already.

Using her restraints as a rope, she swung herself downward, and from side to side. A thick cable was suspended across the chasm between the two wings of the structure. She let go, and with a supreme effort, grabbed it. Now she was within reach of the unconscious man.

With that platform of his about to give way, and only half a frayed harness left, she gave him all of about five seconds. Which gave her three...

"Here...goes...nothing!" she cried, as she let go, dropping onto his platform. She grabbed the man's arm just as the restraints snapped. "Hank McCoy," she muttered under her breath, thinking of her friend Beast, who was an expert at these kinds of maneuvers, "wherever you are, I hope you're smiling."

Another thick cable hung just below the platform. Jean held fast to the man's forearm, and jumped. Just then, an explosion rocked the platform. It broke loose from the structure, and fell into the oblivion of black smoke and orange fire below.

Jean grabbed the cable with her free arm. Now, below her, she could feel the man stirring in her grip, returning to consciousness. And despite the deafening noise, the violent heat, and the thick black smoke that threatened to engulf them both—despite all that, she *knew*. They both knew, the instant they touched.

"A real close shave there...Jean," the man said.

"Scott!!" Jean gasped.

"Yeah, it's me," he told her. "But what I'd like to know is, where are we? And what are we doing in these bodies?!"

Scott did look entirely different. He was older and plainer, with wavy, light brown hair and more thick-set features than his own. But until that moment, it hadn't occurred to Jean that she, too, must look totally different.

But there was no time to think about that now, with explosions still echoing all around them. She helped Scott up to where he, too, could get a grip on the cable. Then, the two of them shimmied down toward the superstructure of the building, and—at least for the moment—safety.

✦   ✦   ✦

While the newlywed couple scrambled to shelter, the people of the city, far below the battle, went about their daily business. Few of them even glanced upward at the sight of the assault upon the Askani Cloisters. The immense structure reached far into the clouds, perched on a high cliff, remote from the rest of the city's business.

For five decades it had stood as a challenge to Apocalypse's rule over the land. Everyone knew that Apocalypse would send his troops to destroy it sooner or later.

Almost two thousand years to the day Jean Grey and Scott Summers had pledged their love to each other, Apocalypse, He-Who-Never-Dies, had decided that the final day of the Askani Sisterhood had arrived.

Jean and Scott stood in a hallway of polished metal. Parts of the walls had been blasted open, and they had to pick their way forward through the rubble. If they fell through the gaps in the floor, they would topple thousands of feet to the ground below.

In the reflection of the shiny metal walls, they inspected their new features. Jean, while still red-headed, was much plainer. She seemed older, too, and so did Scott. Both of them now had faces and bodies that were entirely unremarkable.

"Scott," she said as they leapt down through a hole in the floor to a lower level of the complex, "any chance your new body has optic blasts?"

"Doesn't seem to," he replied, frowning as an explosion went off nearby. "Why? Do you think we'll need them?"

"Just a hunch," she said with a smile. He might look different, but she'd know Scott anywhere. But the smile vanished when they came to another hole in the floor, and saw a company of heavily armed soldiers below them.

"Good hunch," Scott whispered, as they crouched at the hole's edge to watch.

The troop of half a dozen soldiers, holding futuristic-looking blasters raised for combat, was clearly conducting some kind of mopping-up operation. They were led by a fierce-looking man with long orange hair. Around them lay the bodies of what must have been the defenders of the complex.

"You have your orders, everyone," the commander was saying. "Now that the child has been found, every one of these traitors is expendable."

"But sir," one of the soldiers piped up, "it appears they're dead already."

"Then be creative!" the commander snapped. "For years, the many humans below have drawn strength from the tenants of Askani Clan. We'll see how loud and long they cheer when the remains of their precious saviors are draped about the City Forum!"

Jean didn't have any idea what they were talking about, but she'd heard two words that hit her like thunderbolts—Askani and child. The mysterious young woman who'd taken Nathan Christopher with her into the future had called herself Askani. Could this be where she had taken Nate? And if it was, was Nate the child the commander was referring to—the one he'd said had been captured?

Jean tried to contact Scott telepathically. *Scott?*

Jean? his answer came back, much to her surprise. Having lost her telekinetic powers, she'd assumed her telepathic ones were gone as well.

It seems that, despite everything, we've maintained our psionic bond, she told him.

Suppose it makes sense, he replied silently. *Whoever placed us in these bodies filled them with our essences. You and I were a part of each other long before we got married.*

Their telepathic conversation was suddenly interrupted by one of the soldiers below. "Sir," he cried out urgently.

"Shut up," the commander ordered, "and start dragging these bodies down to the surface transport!"

"But that's just it, sir," the soldier insisted. "I'm bio-scanning two survivors!"

Uh-oh, Jean flashed to Scott. *Looks like we've been discovered.*

"What?" the commander shouted. "Where, you gene-dropping son of a flatscan?!"

"There!" the soldier said, pointing straight up at Scott and Jean. "In the rafters!"

The commander looked up and saw them. A sneering grin spread across his face.

"Ah, yes," he said, his eyes narrowing. "Right you are, soldier. There are survivors— but not for long!"

Jean quickly glanced at Scott. *Should we rush them?* she asked him telepathically.

You have to ask? was his reply.

On three...

Chapter 3

Down below, the commander of Apocalypse's troops had a new thought. "Weapons down, everyone!" he ordered. "Powers at the ready! Mother Cromwell's favorite son didn't become part of Apocalypse's elite to spend his career on clean-up duty! Once I pull the secrets of their sacred clan from their bleeding lips, Apocalypse will be…"

His hand shot out, pointing in Jean and Scott's direction, glowing with red light. Then suddenly, before he could use his powers on them, the commander himself was blasted from behind.

As his forces watched, the commander was vaporized in an orange ball of flame. In seconds, all that remained of him were the two skulls that had hung from his weapons belt as trophies of battles past.

"Sir?!"

"Man, that was disgusting," one of his mutant troops remarked with a grimace. The entire troop cowered against the walls of the cloister as an old woman stepped forward. She had short white hair and wore long magenta robes.

"Apocalypse is a fool," she said. Just the sound of the woman's voice sent shock waves through Jean as she listened.

"He's been a fool, in all his different disguises, for as long as I've known him," the old woman continued. "All of which speaks ill of his followers."

She walked slowly toward the cowering mutant troops. "Leave now and you shall live," she said slowly.

"B-by the lips of our master!" one of the troops stammered. He had blue hair and sharp, pointed teeth. "The reports said she was killed in the first wave!"

A female soldier with blue skin and red hair cut him off. "Then the reports were wrong!" she snapped. "Quickly, everyone. On my command, we attack as one!"

"Then alas, children," the old woman said with a sigh, "I fear you'll die as one. For though there was a time I could easily disarm you with but a thought, the years have robbed me of my ability to be subtle."

And now, as the old woman blasted the troop of Apocalypse's soldiers into oblivion, Jean was sure she knew who had come to their aid. *Scott!* she psi-signaled to him. *Our rescuer, i-is...Rachel?*

The old woman turned towards her and looked at her tenderly. *Shush, Mom,* she signaled telepathically. *Not another word until I've taken us away from here where we can—*

But suddenly, before the old woman who was Rachel Summers could explain any further, she found herself enveloped in strong purple tendrils shot at her from behind.

"Wha—? A psionic cocoon!" she gasped. "After all that's happened, I'm too weak to fight it!"

"Consider yourself twice blessed, Mother Askani!" The voice that answered her came from the shadows behind her. It was deep, strong, and powerful, and it belonged to an immense man in green armor, with skulls dangling from his weapons belt and an enormous blaster in his right hand. His blond hair was swept back and upward, resting on his head like a crown.

"My understanding," he continued, smacking her head so hard with the back of his hand that it snapped backward with a crack, "was, you were killed during the first wave of our ambush upon your home! Yet, a closer look reveals barely a scratch on you! Apparently you enjoy making Apocalypse's soldiers appear to be idiots—by causing them to believe they cut you in two with their weapons?"

"Not at all, Ch'vayre," Rachel, the Mother Askani, answered him. "There are still mutants upon this Earth that don't believe having genetic attributes entitles them to—URRNGH!!"

Her words were rudely cut off by another blow, which sent her reeling backward.

"What you or I 'believe' doesn't matter, traitor!" the man called Ch'vayre shouted. "All that truly matters is the law of Apocalypse! It has always been a mystery to me—why he has put up with the existence of your petty religious order for as long as he has. For years, you and your Sisters have catered to the needs of humans and mutants and synthetics…even androids were not beneath your 'standards.' Instead of offering them the hope of a better world—you should have taught your followers to accept the world the way it is! Mutants rule—and only those of us who are the strongest...survive!"

Ch'vayre towered over Rachel, who lay sprawled on the ground beneath his feet. "You, Mother Askani," he went on, his eyes glaring pitilessly down on her, "you and your entire clan of sycophants...have just become extinct!"

Jean and Scott stood frozen, unable to fight back without their vanished mutant powers.

But, as Ch'vayre leveled his blaster at the helpless Rachel, Jean sprang into action to save her daughter from an alternate time line.

Jean? Scott psi-signaled her as she prepared to leap down.

I'm sorry, Scott, she replied silently. *I have to. Umm, cover me?*

And with that, she jumped down from the rafters and landed right in front of Apocalypse's captain. "Hold it, Ch'vayre!" she shouted. "That woman is under my protection!"

Ch'vayre, startled, lowered his blaster and stared at her incredulously. "And you arrrre...?" he asked, drawing out his words.

"A friend," Jean said simply.

"Well then, 'friend,'" Ch'vayre said with a

hideous smile, "in your next life, I'd suggest you take greater care in establishing your alliances. As it is, you have chosen to enlist your services to a broken and dead religious order."

"Yes, well—where there's life, there's hope," Jean said, lamely striking out at him with her fists.

They did no damage at all. "Really?" Ch'vayre taunted her, sneering. "I've never found that to be true."

Scott had been right to hang back, Jean now realized. This attack was suicidal. Until she learned what new powers came with this body of hers, she was nothing more than a moment's distraction to this powerful warrior.

She continued to flail away. "If you insist on pursuing this charade," Ch'vayre said, "let us at least scan your genslate for future reference." He held out a flashing Cerebro-type object in her direction, observing the readout on its tiny monitor. "Hmmm...I'm impressed. You're willing to sacrifice your life for a mutant. It's not what I'd expect...of a human."

Jean froze in mid-punch. "Human?! Are you serious?!" The thought that someone—their own daughter, perhaps—had transported them who knew where...without any powers, was almost more than Jean could comprehend.

"Nice try, flatscan," Ch'vayre said, laughing as his fist flashed out and sent Jean reeling. "You even looked surprised."

But now it was Ch'vayre's turn to be surprised. Scott leapt down to come to the aid of his wife and daughter. He rolled into the back of Ch'vayre's knees, knocking the enormous mutant off balance for the briefest of moments.

"Now what?" Ch'vayre asked. As he recovered, he saw Scott for the first time. "I had long suspected this place was crawling with vermin—I just assumed they weren't of the *Homo inferior* variety."

But Scott, human though he now seemed to be, still had a few tricks up his sleeve. "Lesson number one," he told Ch'vayre as he grabbed the warrior's ankles and rolled sideways, "never underestimate your opponent, Ch'vayre—it's a sign of poor upbringing."

Scott's remark enraged the giant. He roared in anger, and swung his arm, slamming it into Scott's head so hard that he saw stars. "I was raised in the gene-caste where all the gifted are taken!" he bellowed. "Such insults are punishable by death!"

"Whoa! Relax, old man," Scott said, dragging himself erect again. "Where I come from, that was barely an insult."

"Where you come from is the sewers, flatscan," Ch'vayre shot back. "The very spot to which I will return your soon-to-be-decaying corpse!"

Picking Scott up with one hand, he threw him a good twenty feet into the hard, metallic wall. Leveling his blaster, Ch'vayre took two steps forward. "Beg me," he said, "and perhaps I will kill you sooner."

"Well..." Scott said, noticing that he had fallen among the debris of Rachel's assault on the 'dog-soldiers,' "we'll both die of boredom before that day comes, Ch'vayre."

He reached behind him with one hand, feeling something hard and cold...metal. "In all your years of supremacy," he told the gigantic mutant, "you may have forgotten—if you ever knew—that a 'mutant' is nothing more than a human who has learned to change. To adapt to his environment."

And that was exactly what Scott did. Danger Room 101, Lesson One, he remembered from his school days—"Make do with what you have." For example, the remains of a dog-soldier's weapon.

Without warning, Scott whipped the blaster around, already firing at the startled Ch'vayre.

"Sorry about the sucker punch," Scott said, "but it's not as if you went out of your way to be polite before you ambushed my daughter!"

"Daughter?!" Ch'vayre gasped in a choked, garbled voice as the blaster sent him flying into the air. "The Mother Askani is—? Arrggh!" They were his last words before he hit the wall and lost consciousness.

"Rest now, Ch'vayre," Scott told his unconscious foe. "We can talk later."

Looking over at Rachel, he saw that Jean was already helping the old woman to her feet. The psionic cocoon Ch'vayre had cast about her had vanished when he blacked out. But Rachel was still weak—terrifyingly weak, in fact.

"Quickly," she gasped, "we must leave here before it's—"

"No!" Jean insisted. "You're in no position to be moved, Rachel. We'll fight if we—"

"Shush, child," the Mother Askani commanded softly. "You're speaking nonsense to an old woman who has not the time for it. Many people risked everything they had to bring the two of you two thousand years into your future. Please," she begged as Jean held her in her arms, "don't throw away their hopes and dreams on my behalf."

"Two thousand...?" Jean repeated, astonished.

"I'm sorry," Rachel responded in a bare whisper. "I would have asked first...but you being my parents and all...I didn't think you'd mind." She gave Jean a wry smile.

"Is there a way out of this place?" Jean asked her. "Before Ch'vayre wakes?"

"Through this portal," Rachel replied. She raised her arm and pointed at the wall. As if by magic, a mystical door opened in the blue-gray metal. "All of us," she said, with a look at Scott.

"I'll bring up the rear—" he started to say.

"All of us, Scott," Rachel overruled him. "Together."

And nothing more was said.

Chapter 4

Rachel's reason for leading them away from the upper part of the complex was immediately obvious. The tunnel she now led them through was but one of countless tunnels woven throughout the Askani Cloisters. Traveling through the tunnels was difficult at best, as Scott and Jean soon found out. After a long slide down the last of several tubes, they found themselves dumped into neck-high, filthy water.

They must have traveled a mile straight down, Scott realized to his astonishment. For all her power, it seemed that Rachel was scared of something.

No words were necessary. The horrible smell made their location obvious. The three of them were in the sewers!

Scott carried Rachel in his arms, for she was too weak to walk. They moved into shallower water, no more than knee-deep.

Rachel tried to speak, but Scott stopped her.

"Rest now," Scott told her. "Later you can tell us—"

"There'll be no 'later,'" Rachel warned him. "Not for me. Not for the rest of the world."

He let her down onto an outcropping where at least it was dry.

"Best way to sum it up," she said, "is that two millennia after you and the X-Men first defeated him, Apocalypse is triumphant." Her hands reached out, projecting light and...an image. A holographic image of a huge suit of armor, and inside it...

"He looks like—" Jean said.

"A human, Jean?" Rachel finished for her. "Yes. This is his most recent vessel. Just as I am...was...the final vessel of the Phoenix Force."

Jean thought back, remembering vividly her own involvement with the incredibly powerful Phoenix Force. It had taken her form, and it had produced Rachel, too.

"Nearly eighty years ago," Rachel went on, "the Phoenix Force left my old and fragile frame, to search for more fertile ground, I suppose. It is fortunate...even residue of the force is still…impressive."

"But how did you get here?" Scott asked. "Last we saw you—"

"Was at your wedding, yes," Rachel said, nodding. "Upon arriving home in this time, almost a hundred years ago, I found that Apocalypse reigned supreme. The Age of Mutants he had always dreamed of was here. Savage, cruel, powerful mutants did whatever they wanted with their human underlings."

"Wasn't there anyone to stand against them?" Jean asked.

"You have to understand," Rachel told her gently, "for almost a century before this, the world enjoyed racial harmony. The Age of Xavier was a time when all races lived in peace. A peace Apocalypse used against an unsuspecting planet. The people had their will badly battered by the time I'd arrived. I began the Clan Askani. In today's language it means 'family of outsiders.' The closest thing I could come up with that sounded like 'X-Men.'"

Rachel sighed deeply. "As I catered to the sick, I observed that every few years Apocalypse took on a new form. And spent less and less time in each new manifestation, as if he were…burning them out…and therein lies the key to his defeat. You see, he'd been looking for a frame that could accommodate his power. He who preached the survival of the fittest was trying desperately to survive.

"And then, it occurred to me...he was trying to hold on...for the perfect vessel. One dear to all our hearts—Nathan Christopher Summers. Which is why I arranged to grab the child first!"

Jean flashed back to the kidnapping of Nathan by Apocalypse. So that was why he'd wanted the child so badly! So that he could merge with the powerful child, and live forever. The memories flooded her, making sense now for the first time.

"But Nathan was desperately ill," Rachel went on. "I did what I could to save him from the ravages of the techno-organic virus with which Apocalypse had infected him. But time was running out. So as a fail-safe, we created a healthy clone.

"Once Apocalypse figured out Nathan was in this time line, I knew he'd become desperate and attack Askani Hold. You see, together, a cured Nathan and I would have ultimately had the power to overthrow Apocalypse. It is clear now," she concluded with another deep sigh, "that day will never come to pass. Which is why, Jean and Scott—Mom and Dad—I sent for you. You're our last hope."

Jean and Scott looked at each other apprehensively. Without their powers, they knew they stood little chance of successfully battling Apocalypse and his minions.

"But to accomplish your goal," Rachel said, anticipating their thoughts, "you'll need the proper tools. As you've already discovered, the bodies you currently possess—and will possess for your entire stay here—were provided by cloning DNA remains the sisterhood gathered from your descendants. They are as genetically similar to your original bodies as possible. They even have some of your usual powers.

"Unfortunately, with my own power fading, there is a limit to the degree I can re-create those powers—the ones you had in your own bodies. Those bodies would never have survived the time jump arranged by myself and the Clan Askani. But your bodies will become available again after Cabl—I mean, Nathan—has defeated Apocalypse."

"Nathan?" Scott asked. "Where is he?"

"Moments ago," Rachel told them, "he was spirited away from the massacre above by a synthcon named Boak, an old friend of mine. You will find them, no doubt, at a safe house in the upper region."

Jean reached out to grab Rachel as she began to pitch forward, her strength ebbing. "Rachel," she said, "you must be in incredible pain. Please, let us help you."

"You cannot, dear Jean," Rachel said. "For if I am to be any use to you at all...it will not be on this plane of existence. My time is...growing near...for, without the Phoenix Force, Rachel Summers is not much longer for this Earth. Now go, quickly—before Ch'vayre..."

"Rachel? No!" Jean screamed, as her daughter fainted dead away in her arms. The feelings of motherhood were startling—and unfamiliar.

"Oh, Scott," she said tearfully, "in our own era, it's been hardly a week since Rachel and I reconciled. And here I am, with her comatose body in my arms! It can't end this way, Scott!"

"It won't, Jean," he said hoarsely, his arms on her shoulders. "I promise."

It had been less than a week—and two thousand years ago—when this couple made a similar promise to one another. To love, honor, and cherish each other—every day for the rest of their lives. Having taken their vows in front of friends and family, they'd left for a tropical paradise to honeymoon in privacy. And then, the Clan Askani had summoned them, with a call that echoed across the ages.

Five of the Askani Sisters had ignored the pain and bloodshed and chaos of Apocalypse's assault, to bring Scott and Jean Summers forward through the centuries.

What had become of their original bodies, emptied of mind and soul as they swam in the shallow waters off the beach on St. Bart's? They had no idea. And right now, they didn't want to think about it.

Jean wandered ahead about fifty feet from where Scott stood, holding Rachel's limp body in his arms. She stopped to stare out a gap in the walls and called to him, "Scott, I think you should see this."

He walked over to her and looked out at the utterly strange world that was now the Earth. The sky was purple and red, fading to orange near the horizon. Strange, lifelike structures towered into the sky—buildings, he realized. The waters of the Askani sewers poured over the edge of the cloister in a cascade that disappeared far below.

"It's all so different now," Jean said.

"Yeah," he agreed. "The landscape is un-recognizable. If not for Rachel, I'd doubt we were even on—"

"I'm not talking about the view," Jean interrupted. "I'm talking about the perspective. Since the day we first slipped into those blue and gold jumpsuits at the professor's school, we've faced everything the world had to throw at us. There were times, I'll admit now, when I was nervous. Times when I was surprised. And—once in a great while—scared.

"But this is different," she continued. "The professor, Storm, Warren...everyone we ever knew—ever loved—is gone. We've spent years risking our lives for a world that feared us because of what we were...not a lot of fun, no—but at least it was *our* world, Scott. Our lives. But we're so far into the future, we might as well be on another planet entirely!"

"You're forgetting one thing, Jean," Scott replied solemnly. "The one thing that hasn't changed. Our love for each other."

They turned and gazed into each other's eyes, feeling the rush of love between them.

"My human friends," a voice rang out, "why do you delay the inevitable?"

Chapter 5

It was Ch'vayre!

"I ask you again," the voice boomed out from a platform high above them, "why do you delay the inevitable? If you agree to spare all of us the time it will take to track you down, I might be able to arrange your deaths at the hands of Lord Apocalypse himself. Think of the glory!"

How positively generous of the guy, Scott psi-signaled Jean. The two of them stood in the knee-deep water, Scott still holding the unconscious Rachel in his arms.

Scott could barely make out the silhouette of Apocalypse's captain, he stood so high above them. Behind him, bright searchlights scanned the lower levels of the complex. Obviously, while Ch'vayre knew they were somewhere in the area, he had not yet pinpointed their location. He was simply calling out to them, assuming they could hear him, hoping they would surrender without a fight. Fat chance!

Ch'vayre appeared to be surrounded by dozens of mutant soldiers. Below them, on an intermediate level of the complex between the sewers and Ch'vayre's high platform, another patrol prowled the darkness, blasters at the ready.

"It must be clear to you by now," he shouted down in their general direction, "that the House of the Askani has fallen! Just as the Xavier Collective fell before that—and the Scions of Genetics before that—and the X.S.E. before them! Only Apocalypse remains. Only his vision of a world where the strongest survive!"

Ch'vayre's tirade was interrupted by one of his soldiers, who came up behind him, a look of confusion on his face. "Sir," he said, "the cerebral imprints I've been trailing have suddenly gone cold. Working under the assumption I'm being psionically blindsided, I suggest a bio-anomaly scan of this quadrant."

"That won't be necessary," Ch'vayre told him, his voice echoing off the walls loudly enough for Scott and Jean to hear him. "Even if Mother Askani is still alive after all this, she would be much too weak to jam your scan. And I've already established that her would-be saviors are humans."

He waved his hand impatiently. "No," he said. "This is getting tedious. We should be celebrating with our Lord, instead of wading through the sewers. This man and woman, whoever they are, have already shown an affinity for the weak and helpless. Come," he commanded. "Bring forth the child!"

"The child," Scott whispered, a shudder running through him as he held Rachel tighter.

Shhh, Scott, Jean warned him telepathically. *My powers apparently aren't as developed in this body. It's all I can do to mentally block an awareness of the three of us. You mustn't speak out loud!*

Above them, Ch'vayre held the tiny child aloft. The infant was barely bigger than the enormous hand of the mutant commander. "I propose an exchange," he bellowed. "A new life for an old one! This infant was torn from the grip of a wounded synthcon who counted himself among the Clan Askani's supporters— so I'm assuming it holds some significance for you people. Step forward...lay the dying, broken body of your sacred Mother before us—

and the boy is yours!"

Scott, Jean signaled. *Is it—?*

I can't tell, Jean, he silently replied. *Not from here. Can't even tell if the child is still alive.*

But now, suddenly, the platform on which Ch'vayre was standing began to move, gliding through the air! Scott could see that it was not part of the structure of the complex at all, but rather, a large hovercraft, with searchlights attached, on which Ch'vayre rode with his lieutenants. They floated over dozens of his soldiers, who were traipsing through the muck and water in search of their quarry.

The hovercraft sank lower, and came closer and closer to the spot where Scott, Jean, and Rachel hid.

"Soon," Ch'vayre called out in his booming voice, still holding the infant aloft in his upraised hand, "these tunnels will be filled to overflowing with hundreds of soldiers loyal to Apocalypse. I am offering you the opportunity to leave here with one of your own—a human. Flawed. Scarred. Afflicted. But a human nonetheless."

He held the child in the glow of the searchlights. And now, it was clear what Ch'vayre was talking about. The child's face and body were scarred—infested—with techno-organic matter, tendrils and microcircuitry that had once been flesh.

This was a sight Scott had felt sure he'd never see again in all his life. The sight of his infant son, Nathan Christopher Summers.

Jean must have sensed the rising fury and longing inside him. *Scott,* she warned him telepathically, *you know he's baiting us!*

Jean, that's Nathan! he retorted. *Just like he was, when I was forced to send him to this future in order to save his life! One Ch'vayre, or one thousand—nothing's going to keep us apart!*

I wasn't suggesting otherwise, Jean told him. *Just pointing out the obvious. On three, then?*

No! Scott insisted. *Take Rachel and find a way out! The four of us will meet up later.*

Scott, come back! Jean ordered, freezing him in his tracks for a moment, just as he began to slog through the sewer in Ch'vayre's direction. *You don't even know what you're working with. You're already too far out of my range for me to psionically mask your presence!*

He turned to look at her for a brief moment. *Give me a telekinetic lift to Ch'vayre, then go!* he demanded.

No way, Scott, she held firm. *We're in this*

together—till death do us part, remember?

She gave him the lift all right—but she didn't take Rachel and go. Instead, she stood below, watching, as Scott flew up through the darkness. Her powers had returned, all right. But they were still not perfectly under her control.

Whoa! he signaled Jean. *You didn't have to throw me quite this hard!*

"Ch'vayre—look!" one of his lieutenants shouted, pointing to Scott as he flew toward them.

Luckily, Scott righted himself just in time, kicking the blaster from the lieutenant's hand just as it fired.

Ch'vayre looked on, furious yet impressed. "Slamming into my men with enough force to shatter every bone in your body, hmmm?" he said. "What an 'interesting' fighting technique. Desperate, yet effective."

He handed Nathan to another lieutenant. "Take the child, Aurron," he ordered.

"Yes, m'lord," the lieutenant complied.

Ch'vayre turned to Scott, baring his teeth. "I confess to being surprised you didn't leave when you had the chance to survive," he said, raising his hand and pointing it at Scott, ready to strike.

But Scott was ready for him. "You're the one who should stick around, Ch'vayre," he said. "I haven't even begun to surprise you!"

And with that, he leveled an optic blast straight at Apocalypse's commander, sending him reeling backward toward the edge of the giant hovercraft.

"Wha—!? Your eyes!" Ch'vayre gasped in astonishment. "B-but the readings indicated you were not a—URNNGH!"

Again he flew backward, this time losing his footing and toppling off the edge of the platform, into the muck below!

"Lesson number two!" Scott called after him. "Don't believe everything you read!"

"This is insane!" Ch'vayre shrieked, rising from the water as Scott blasted away at the other occupants of the hovercraft. "No one has opposed the will of Apocalypse in nearly a hundred years—let alone another m-mutant?"

"Times change," Scott called down to him, as he grabbed Nathan from Aurron's grasp. With another optic blast, he sent the lieutenant flying through the darkness. "Believe me—times change. And every once in a while, they change for the better."

The infant looked up at him, his eyes widening. "Daa...?" he mouthed.

"Yes, Nate," Scott told him, his heart melting with love for his child. "Daddy's here."

Scott, Jean signaled him from down below, *you know no one could be happier for you. But we've got to get moving if we're going to be holding any family reunions any time soon. And while it looks like you've gained a lot more control over this version of your optic blasts...*

He looked down and saw that she was using her own telekinetic powers to keep the dozens of soldiers coming toward her and Rachel at bay.

Ignore them! Scott instructed her.

Huh? she asked, thinking he must be joking. *There's an idea I wouldn't have thought of on my own.*

I'm serious! he insisted. *Concentrate on throwing open the drainage pipes!*

And flood the chamber with all the water all at once? she asked. Suddenly she grasped his meaning, and saw the brilliance of his plan. *I knew there was a reason I agreed to obey you!* she told him, raising her hand and causing all the drainage ducts to pour forth their contents. Millions of gallons rushed into the sewers at once, causing panic among the soldiers.

But you didn't agree to obey me, Scott reminded her as he leapt down to join her, with Nathan still in his arms. *You specifically had it written out of the marriage vows!* he joked. Jean clung to Rachel, and the four of them floated downstream. The soldiers behind them panicked, drowning in their heavy metallic armor as the rushing torrent overwhelmed them.

True, Jean agreed. *But that was for another reason entirely.*

Jean, please, Scott signaled, managing to smile at her as they were swept along. *Not in front of the children!*

See you down below, Scott? she replied as they approached the waterfall looming up ahead.

It's a date, he agreed.

And then, the rushing water engulfed them in its churning frenzy.

It was nearly half an hour later that the flash flood died down. There was only one survivor among Apocalypse's soldiers—Ch'vayre himself.

He had spent the entire time clinging to

the ruined walls of the Askani Cloister.

"Man...woman...whoever you are—" he swore under his breath as he dragged himself out of the muck and looked at the corpses of his drowned men strewn all around, "wherever you go, know that this is not over. In the name of Apocalypse," he swore, his voice rising to a shout that echoed off the walls, "I will be avenged!"

But his angry curse could not be heard above the roar of the still-raging water.

Twenty miles downstream along the shoreline, Scott and the infant Nathan Christopher emerged from the water, drenched, exhausted—but alive.

"Made it!" Scott gasped exultantly, staring all around him at the barren, mountainous wilderness which loomed on all sides. Then he looked down at the child in his arms. Nate's eyes were closed, and he appeared to be sleeping!

"Made it—and the kid slept through the whole thing? Amazing."

"Wonder whose side of the family he gets that from?" Jean asked, climbing out of the water behind him, dragging Rachel along with her.

"Jean—you're here?!" Scott said, limping over to give her a hand. His knee hurt—he must have injured it in the waterfall—but the adrenaline coursing through him allowed him to ignore the pain, at least for the moment. "I was afraid it would take weeks to find each other again!"

"Not likely, Mr. Summers," she told him, flashing him a grin. "Fortunately, our bond allowed Rachel and me to stay telekinetically tethered to the two of you."

"Is she all right?" Scott asked anxiously.

"As near as I can tell, she's in a coma," Jean told him, her face grave. "I'm not able to detect anything active within her mind."

She looked deeply into her husband's eyes. "It looks as though it's official," she said soberly. "If we're going to pull this off—raise Nathan, overthrow Apocalypse, and liberate all the races enslaved in this era—it's entirely up to you and me."

Scott returned her gaze, nodding in agreement. "To tell you the truth, Mrs. Summers," he said, "if we accomplish even half of that— I'd say we had a fairly productive honeymoon."

Chapter 6

They were hot...exhausted...hungry. But none of that mattered, for they were together.

The boy, now almost six years old, rested in the woman's arms as she rode the tired old horse along the high road. The man walked beside them, leaning on the walking stick he'd used since he'd injured his knee five years ago. It still hurt occasionally, but not too badly. He insisted on walking while the others rode. Their few possessions fit easily into the saddle-bags the horse carried.

Other travelers passed them as they paused by the side of the road to rest for a moment. The man shielded his eyes from the sun and gazed into the hazy distance. It was already afternoon. The day was sunny and hot, and they were still far from their destination.

"Redd?" the boy asked sleepily.

"Yes, Nate?" the woman replied.

"Are we almost there yet?"

It was the man who answered. "We're exactly where we're supposed to be. We're home, Nate. We're home."

According to their transit disks, the unit designate, Dayspring, had been traveling for three weeks: "Permission granted by Lord Apocalypse's Interprovince Pilgrimage Council for tertiary migration: Cloister Shade to the Citadel of Crestcoast."

Over the past five years, Slym and Redd Dayspring, as Scott and Jean now called themselves, had hidden themselves among the Sapien, or human, caste. They had lived hand to mouth, fleeing from town to town, province to province, making any sacrifice necessary to ensure the safety of the child destined to free an entire world from genetic oppression.

They rounded another bend in the highway, and suddenly, across a spectacular chasm, the Citadel of Crestcoast loomed before them. It rose along the chasm walls on the far side, towering over the raging river at the canyon's bottom. Its futuristic, metallic vastness made it look like an alien space city. Slym had to keep reminding himself that he and the others were still on Earth.

A long bridge below them spanned the chasm, but the road down to it was steep, hugging the cliff precariously. Scott helped Nate down off the horse, and Jean got down, too. They would all have to walk the rest of the way to the bridge.

"This is our third home this year, Slym," Nate complained as he let Scott help him down. "Every time I start fun-bonding, we start routing again."

"Crestcoast has been our destination all along, Nate," Jean told him. "Now that we're here, we'll be able to settle down for a while."

"But I liked the other place better!" Nate insisted. "And the place before and—"

Jean interrupted him, putting a hand on his shoulder. "The law says," she said, "that every ten years, every non-mutant must return to the city of his or her origin for a genetic scan. Give it a chance—this might turn out to be the best place to live."

"Yeah, firm," Nate said skeptically. "We're humans—we'll never live anyplace nice."

Jean took his hand, but a faraway look had come into her eyes. Nate noticed it, and bit his lip. "Redd," he asked, "have you and Slym ever thought about dumping me—like my real parents did—so that, y'know, my diseases wouldn't make it harder for you to fit in?"

He looked up at her, and she returned his gaze with a smile. The skin around his right eye had given way to techno-organic matter, as had almost his entire left arm. The disease's progress had slowed since Nate's infancy, but Jean knew that it embarrassed him greatly. Other children teased him, and their parents kept them away from him.

"Oh, sure," Jean told him in a wry tone. "We might try to trade you in for something real useful—like a blender."

"Ulp," Nate swallowed hard. "You're teasing, right?"

"Mostly," Jean admitted, giving his hand a squeeze.

"Chee hee," Nate giggled, relieved. "So... what's a blender?" he asked.

Walking behind the two of them, Scott smiled contentedly. He knew that two thousand years had passed since anyone had heard of a blender.

Amazing, he thought. *After all they'd been through, they'd managed to stay together as a family.*

In many ways, that family had begun on

the day he'd married Jean Grey. Yet in many other ways, this particular branch of the Summers family tree began years before that happy event.

On the darkest day of his young life, Scott Summers had allowed a novitiate of the Clan Askani to take his infant son, Nathan Christopher, far into the future in order to cure the boy of his deadly techno-organic virus. That most heart-wrenching of decisions would not have been any easier had he known then what he knew now—that his own time-lost daughter, Rachel, was, in fact, the sacred Mother Askani. Or that she had founded this new religion, and sought to save Nathan Christopher, so that one day he would destroy Apocalypse and liberate an enslaved planet as the man called Cable.

"Arngh!" Scott cried out as he stepped into a small depression in the dirt roadway, turning his ankle and reinjuring his knee. Jean and Nate, walking ahead of him, heard his cry and came back to help him to his feet again.

The trip through time had landed Scott in another body—one which allowed him control over his optic blasts for the first time in his life. Ironically, he had not been here even one hour when he'd wrenched his knee in the fall from Askani Hold. In the frenzy of their escape, he hadn't noticed it until he'd come out of the water and tried to walk. But it was taking a long time to heal.

But it was a small price to pay, Scott decided, for a man to finally have his son.

Jean and Nate asked if he was all right, forgetting in their concern to disguise their speech as they usually did when others were around. A bearded man walking a horse even older than their own stopped beside them.

"Ill met, fellow traveler?" he asked Scott, who was leaning against the horse, waiting for the pain in his knee to abate.

"I am fine, thank you," Scott told him, not at all eager to make conversation with a stranger. Apocalypse's spies were everywhere, and one had to choose one's friends carefully, even among the Sapien caste.

"I could not help but notice," the man said, "your unit speaks Old English—no?"

"N-no," Scott stammered, caught off guard. "Perhaps you heard us incorrectly."

"Perhaps," the man said dubiously. "G'journey," he added as he walked off down the road toward the citadel.

"G'journey," Scott called after him.

"Uh-oh," Jean whispered. "Trouble?"

"Could be," Scott whispered back. "Jean, we have to be more careful."

"You tripped over a rock, Scott."

"I'm talking about using what they call Old English in front of other people," he explained. "We might find it more comfortable. But it marks us as outsiders when we're trying hard to fit in. For the moment, Jean, when we need privacy, we'll communicate through our psychic rapport. Remember, the entire reason we're hiding out here among the humans is to raise Nathan out from under the eye of Apocalypse's ruling class."

Jean switched to telepathic communication at once. *The same reason we're 'returning' to Crestcoast,* she added. *Because the fractured remnants of the Askani Clan came up with documentation which puts us squarely and safely in the lowest caste of humans. Funny, though,* she added, gazing up into his eyes, *I don't feel like the lowest caste.*

They fell into each other's arms and they kissed.

Though their bodies had changed, their love for each other remained the same.

Chapter 7

The House of Apocalypse lay only three hundred miles south of Crestcoast, along a body of water once known as the Pacific Ocean. But for all its wealth, its excess, its corruption, it might as well have been an entire world away.

And most of the mutant ruling class liked it that way. One among them, however, felt differently. He hated the parties that went on, day and night, in the halls of the palace.

His name was Ch'vayre. As he climbed the red-carpeted staircase, mutants in brocaded robes and satin gowns made way for him, bowing to show their respect for his high position. Once he had passed by them, however, they went right back to their revelry, ignoring the scornful, scowling look on his face.

He walked down the marble hallway, which in its luxury and ornate appointments resembled the ancient palace of a Roman emperor.

Soon he came to a vast ballroom, passing under a stone archway with its chiseled likeness of Apocalypse's grinning face.

The ballroom was filled to overflowing with guests. One milling group of mutants turned to witness his entrance. "By Sabah Nur's genes—it's him!" one of them said, her eyes widening in fear at the sight of Ch'vayre.

"Don't fear," said one of the others, a beautiful, red-haired mutant. "I'll handle him."

"It'll not happen," a male mutant standing with them said, shaking his head. "Nobody can handle Prelate Paladin Ch'vayre."

Ch'vayre scanned the crowd that filled the enormous chamber. He was twice the height of any of them. And even without telepathic powers, he could sense their thoughts. It was written plainly on their sniveling faces—they did not like him, any more than he liked them.

"M'honor," the redhead said, approaching him, "might I offer you a moment's alternative to your tortured thoughts?"

Ch'vayre pushed her rudely away from him. "You can offer me nothing, gene trash," he said.

The woman was caught totally off guard. "I—I meant no offense, honored one," she stammered. "I meant only to congratulate you on the anniversary of the extermination of the Askani sect."

Ch'vayre bent down low over the cowering woman. "My thoughts," he told her gruffly, "tortured or otherwise, belong to none but Ch'vayre!"

As did his failures, he thought to himself as the redhead retreated back to her friends. There lay the reason for his anger, did it not? For all his claims of dedication to the Lord Apocalypse—or En Sabah Nur, as he was most often referred to around the palace—the truth was that he, Ch'vayre, had failed his master when Apocalypse had needed him to defeat the last of his enemies—when he'd led the assault on Askani Hold.

A man and a woman had escaped. A small exception to total victory, he'd thought back then. But it had turned out to be one that had cost him dearly. For it had prevented the total disintegration of the Mother Askani's hated fold. Somehow...some way...that couple had managed to carry on the old woman's teachings, allowing them to inspire the lowscans and to frustrate his Lord and Master's plan.

With a sudden flash of light and boom of

sound, a shock wave raced through the ball-room, knocking everyone to the floor. The heat was so intense it took their breath away.

The blast had come from the other side of the great arch—the Master's chamber.

"We are under attack!" one of the fright-ened guests cried out in panic.

"It is the humans—it must be!" shouted another.

"We're to be killed by flatscans!" screamed a third.

Ch'vayre had had enough of their snivel-ing cowardice. "That is impossible!" he bel-lowed, rising to his full, twelve-foot height. "In the name of Apocalypse personified, I order you all to remain calm!"

How repulsive it was, he thought disgust-edly, to watch these pampered children of a sick and diseased aristocracy flee in terror. There had once been a time, not so long ago, when Apocalypse's vision of a world ruled by the survival of the fittest had been just that. But that was before they had become sloppy, fat, and lazy. Before they sank so low that they could be frightened out of their wits by—the tantrum of a child!

For now, through the great archway, came

the boy—with his copper-colored hair, his royal robes and cape, and that perpetual sneer on his young face. He kicked a skull loose from its skeleton. Behind him, one of the young prince's attendants trailed, biting his nails.

"Magal!" Ch'vayre hailed the attendant. "What happened here? What happened to the boy's instructor?"

"That's mostly him on the floor, Prelate Paladin," Magal answered, still chewing on his nails, nervous that he would come to the same fate as the poor tutor. "P-perhaps Stryfe would care to explain to his Lord Ch'vayre what has happened?" he suggested to the boy.

"Explain?" the boy repeated, looking up at Magal. "What is there to explain? He told me 'study.' I told him 'no.' End log."

Ch'vayre bent down over the child, noticing as he did so that the vast ballroom was now totally deserted. The arrival of Stryfe in a room tended to have that effect.

"It is far from an 'end log,' child!" Ch'vayre told the boy. "I have stressed this before—you cannot and must not randomly use your mutant power against anyone who displeases you!"

"But why, Ch'vayre?" the boy asked. "He

was just a low-lev. Not even a full mutation."

"Even low-levs have a right to live, Stryfe," Ch'vayre pointed out. "The word according to Apocalypse speaks not only of 'survival of the fittest'—but no source of mutation may be eliminated without the Holy Word! You have been blessed, child, because you, above all others, have been chosen as his successor. But you do not as yet have the right of extermination."

"I don't feel blessed," the boy said, pouting. "I feel bored. Are you done?"

"No," Ch'vayre shot back angrily. "And I will most assuredly not be done until I have pounded it into your dense skull that—"

"Yes. He's done."

Ch'vayre froze in mid-sentence. His Lord and Master's voice had spoken.

Stryfe smiled innocently. "You were saying, M'Lord Ch'vayre?" he challenged.

"A topic for another time, perhaps," Ch'vayre said through clenched teeth.

"Perhaps," the boy chirped, running past Ch'vayre to the open arms of Apocalypse.

"Come to me, my son," said the ruler of all the Earth. In his blue metallic armor, he was taller even than Ch'vayre. Smiling faces floated on disembodied heads in midair above either shoulder, while techno-organic arms reached out to embrace the boy Stryfe. And in the middle of the suit of armor, Apocalypse himself— now in the guise of a shriveled old man— reached out his withered, frail arms as well.

"Share with me this day's trials and travails," Apocalypse said, embracing the boy.

"Not much to speak of, really," said Stryfe, taking the withered hands in his own. "You know how Ch'vayre gets all sentimentalized over the livestock. It's really quite charming, in an archaic kind of way."

"Be patient with him, child," Apocalypse advised his heir. "He does not have our power...and therefore lacks our perspective. But you, Stryfe, my little Lordling, you can already taste our destiny on your lips—already feel the hunger welling up inside you. Come...know but the shadow of the embrace we shall one day know for the rest of eternity."

"Yes, 'father,'" Stryfe said, allowing the withered arms to embrace him. "Hold me and teach me all the things only one who has lived through the centuries can teach."

"In time, child," Apocalypse promised, stroking the boy's hair. "Now, run along. Find something to amuse yourself with—incinerate another instructor if you must—but I need a moment alone with Ch'vayre."

The boy happily did as he was told. He skipped off through the great archway. *Looking for somebody else to have his bloody fun with,* Ch'vayre thought sadly.

Apocalypse turned to face his prelate. The armor, which had opened to admit the boy to Apocalypse's embrace, now closed over the old man. All Ch'vayre saw were the smiling, disembodied faces of En Sabah Nur.

"You do not like the boy very much, do you, Prelate?" Apocalypse said.

Ch'vayre bowed his head humbly. "My likes or dislikes are unimport—" he began.

But Apocalypse cut him off. "Speak openly, friend," he urged. "It is one of the few aspects of our relationship I still enjoy. Your feelings about the boy?"

Ch'vayre looked carefully at his Lord and Master, trying to decide if the invitation was sincere. He decided that, sincere or not, he would speak his mind.

"As you say," he told Apocalypse. "He is a boy. I believe he should be allowed to grow up in his own time, Lord Apocalypse. By accelerating his mutant abilities, you are going against every one of the laws of natural selection you have lived by since—"

"Since forever, it seems," Apocalypse cut in. "You are right. But I am running out of time. Each new body I inhabit burns out more quickly—the more powerful I have become, the less these pitiful vessels can maintain that power." The armor lifted once more to show the shriveled old man in whose body Apocalypse, for the moment, resided.

"But Stryfe," he went on, "is different. The genetic clone of Scott Summers and Jean Grey's son has survived the techno-organic virus to which he was exposed. He is everything I've ever wanted to be. He is the personification of the tenet of survival of the fittest—and we will survive, Ch'vayre," he finished, turning and gliding through the great arch on the hoverjets which protruded from the armor covering his feet. "*I* will survive..."

But at what cost? Ch'vayre wondered as he watched his master go. Was Apocalypse prepared to stand back and nurture the child, as his empire fell apart around him?

And was he, Ch'vayre, supposed to just sit back and let it happen?

Chapter 8

The boy Nathan Christopher Dayspring looked down at his left arm—the one that usually looked like part of a machine. Now, as he watched in astonishment, skin grew down from the shoulder, covering the metallic cables that were his biceps, the living microcircuits that were taking him over bit by bit. The human skin advanced to the elbow, then kept growing, covering his forearm, his wrist, his hand—until he looked just like any other boy.

"Hyperbolic!" he gasped, wiggling his fingers. "But I don't understand, Redd, how you can use your mind to change the way I look. And it doesn't even hurt much anymore!"

"As I've said before, Nate," she replied, "it's biorhythms. So long as we touch, I can help you control your physical appearance long enough to get us past the city's vanguard."

"Is it true, what you've said?" he asked her,

"that someday I'll be able to control my body myself and pass for normal all the time?"

"Believe me, kid," Slym interjected, "you'll be a lot more than 'normal.'"

"Slym is right, Nate," Redd told the boy, who was giving his 'stepfather' a puzzled look. "You must disguise yourself because there are many people who fear and hate what they don't understand. But there will come a day when you'll be accepted—and respected—for who and what you are."

She hugged him fiercely, then adjusted the round, flat-topped cap he wore on his head, and brushed back his copper-colored hair where it stuck out at the sides. "Until then," she went on, "you'll have to shush so we can make it through the validation checkpoint."

They had crossed the bridge over the chasm and entered the city through its only portal. Now, the three travelers huddled in the shadows of a dead-end alleyway, where Jean could effect Nate's transformation, unseen by curious eyes, before they ventured to the checkpoint that controlled all access into the city proper.

Nate looked worried. "But how will I know when—?" he started to ask.

"Shhhh," Jean warned him, giving his hand a squeeze. Then she signaled him telepathically. *Save question three thousand and three for after dinner.*

He smiled up at her. *That is so rage, when you talk in my brain!* he signaled back.

Together, the Dayspring family unit emerged from the alleyway and headed for the checkpoint. It stood underneath an inner archway, protected by a metal gate that hung from above, ready to drop down at a moment's notice and deny all access to the city.

The checkpoint was manned by a troop of Apocalypse's vanguard—and a sorry-looking troop it was, Scott noticed. He'd known that the Citadel of Crestcoast was a poor, remote outpost, but he hadn't known just how forsaken it would be.

One of the guards rolled his eyes as the ragged family approached the checkpoint. "Dese humans be worse than the lemmings," he remarked to his mutant comrades. "One after de other after de other after—"

"Don't be rude, Bolt," one of the others scolded him, leering at the newcomers. "They're just doing as they've been commanded by the Lord High-Muck-a-Muck

Apocalypse. Can't allow the *Homo inferiors* free reign of the planet. G'journey, traveler," he called out to Scott. "Welcome to the proud city of Crestcoast. 'Tis a pleasure to have you back, I'm certain."

Scott hesitated momentarily. Was he just being paranoid, or had he detected a faint hint of sarcasm in the soldier's tone of voice?

The guard stepped forward and held out his hand, palm upward. "Your unit's credentials?" he demanded.

"Right here, sir," Scott said, handing him the transit disk. "Clan Dayspring and one adoptee."

"Yes, yes," the soldier said impatiently.

He grabbed the disk so roughly that it shattered into a dozen pieces!

"Oops," the guard said, sneering. "Guess I don't know my own strength."

Scott—? Jean signaled him, clearly worried.

I don't know, Jean, he returned her silent communication. *But without referents, we're so much gene fodder! I doubt the remains of the Clan Askani could help us then.*

He turned to the soldier who had destroyed his card. "Honored vanguard—how may we enter the city gates without our papers?" he asked aloud.

A third soldier answered—a fierce-looking mutant with a monster's face and blue hair— with a fist to Scott's jaw! "It's not a human's place to question one of mutant blood!" he roared, as Scott hit the ground with a thud. "Think not just 'cause we been cast among the refuse that we be refuse ourselves!"

"An honest enough mistake on its part," said the soldier who had destroyed Scott's disk. "It assumes that anyone assigned to a rear-water outpost must be the last of Apocalypse's Honor Guard. It thinks we're stupid, Marl. Hit it again. Show it how stupid we are."

The blue-haired soldier complied, dragging Scott to his feet, only to send him staggering backward with another all-out blow to the jaw.

Scott saw, through the haze that enveloped his brain, that these soldiers held a fierce grudge about having been posted to such an undesirable duty. He was at the wrong place at the wrong time.

But Nate didn't see things that way at all. What he saw was Slym, his beloved Slym, being beaten up by a gang of toughs and bullies. It enraged him—and he tried to break free of Jean and join the fight.

"Nate, please..." Jean warned him, holding on to the boy for dear life. She feared that he'd lose contact with her and expose his true appearance for all to see.

"Let go of me!" Nate raged, squirming in a desperate effort to break loose. "Nobody slams Slym while I'm around!"

"Stay out of this, mutt," the soldier who'd broken their disk ordered. "This is between the state and your guardians...who we suspect to be enemies of Apocalypse."

Scott's breath caught in his throat. So this was not some petty grudge after all!

"On what grounds?" he asked them, sitting up. "We have nothing but respect for our genetic overlord!"

The voice that answered him came from the shadows—and it chilled Scott to the bone.

"These people are liars!"

He had heard that voice before—not long ago—but where?

And then the man stepped out of the shadows—the bearded man they had met on the road!

"I heard them speaking Old English on the trail!" he shouted, pointing an accusing finger at Scott. "They would not do so unless they had something to hide!"

The three soldiers surrounded Scott, who still lay prone on the ground, propped up on his elbow. The man with the beard hung back, waiting to see what the soldiers would do with the information he'd given them.

The soldier who had first greeted them now held a bottle in his hand. He clutched it by the neck and obviously meant to use it as a weapon.

The huge, blue-haired soldier named Marl grinned hungrily at Scott. "Sounds suspicious to me," he said, his hands curling into fists. "Twicely so. Hit him again?"

"Not just yet," said the soldier who'd broken their disk, and who seemed to be their leader. "Let us hear what he has to say for himself."

They closed in on him, towering over him, moving in for the kill.

"You couldn't have come at a better time, flatscan," said the first soldier. "We've been waiting for an opportunity to transfer out of dis dump. Tell us what you're hiding, and we'll be our Lord's favorite gene line."

"Talk," said Marl. "And make it good..."

Chapter 9

Scott lay propped on his elbow, staring up at his attackers as they closed in on him. If his main concern hadn't been protecting Nathan, he would have revealed the very mutant abilities he was hiding.

"This is all easily explained," he told the guards in a pleading tone of voice that masked his real feelings. "My mate was raised by the Clan Askani as a servant. I assure you she never believed their tenets." It was a lie, of course—but not bad for an improvisation. "But she is more comfortable speak—"

The monstrous blue mutant growled. "Askani long gone!" he interrupted. "Never spoke garble-guk. Did they?"

"They may have," the guard in charge replied, "but I haven't the slightest. I say we at least take the whole unit before Paladin Ch'vayre and see what he has to say."

"Let's see what's left of de unit—after we have some fun!" the first guard suggested.

"And after I receive my reward, no?" the bearded spy interjected.

"Reward, eh?" the first guard repeated. "Never much liked turncoats, but wha—?"

He turned suddenly, stunned to see that the small boy was rushing at him.

"Nate, no!" Jean shouted.

But it was too late. Nate was acting without thinking—on pure impulse.

"Weave us awone—woser!" he cried, sinking those sharp teeth into the guard's thigh.

"Aieergh! He bit me!" the guard screamed. "This nothing mutt halfscan bit me!" His fist crashed into Nate's face.

"That was nothin'!" Nate cried. "Now, are you gonna let us by, or—oof!" Another blow to the head cut him off in mid-sentence, and Nate fell backward, into Scott's arms.

Scott grabbed him, instinctively. *Go limp, son—I have you,* he signaled telepathically.

Son? Nate repeated, confused.

It's an Old English term, Nate, Scott explained. *I'll explain it someday. For now, I have a more valuable lesson I need to administer.*

The man who had once been known as

Cyclops looked up at the guards who had attacked him and his family. "To be fair, gentlemen," he said, "I should give you one last opportunity to let us pass. Now."

"Not on your filthy lives," the chief guard shot back. "Your unit is clearly our transit out of this dump! The Lord's science staff will spend weeks at the dissection table!"

"What are you talking about, my friend?" Scott asked, totally confused. "What possible interest would we hold for the scientists?"

"Because of *him*," the guard replied, pointing to Nate. "De boy!"

Scott looked down at his frightened child, who clung to him. Nate's arm, freed from Jean's protective grasp, now showed itself in its true, diseased form!

"Sorry, Slym," Nate moaned miserably.

"No problem," Scott told him. "We'll be out of here in a moment, Nate." His eyes began to glow as he readied an optic blast.

"Powers?" the monstrous blue mutant named Marl gasped. "Good!" He moved slowly toward Scott with an evil grin on his face.

The chief of the guards raised his arms and pointed them toward Scott. His hands began to glow with reddish light. "Bad assignment or not, human, we are still your genetic superiors! You cannot stop us from wresting the child from your cold, lifeless fingers."

"Who knows?" the guard with the bottle said, gazing at Nathan. "By the look of him, maybe the mutt is a mutant as well?"

"Stand back, Nathan," Scott warned him, as Jean came forward to stand by his side.

"We'll only be a moment," Jean said, her eyes on the guards.

And then, to everyone's complete surprise, came a voice from above. "Ssssoooner actually...if I havvvve my way."

Marl looked up in panic. "Uh, look, guys," he told his comrades.

"It's Turrin!" the chief guard gasped.

Scott looked up at the man—if he *was* a man. His upper half looked human enough, except for his left arm, which ended in an enormous cannon. And his bottom half was fused into some sort of hovercraft. The man floated silently in the air above them.

His face was somewhat like the spy's—dark, bearded, with short, curly hair—but this face was more noble, more serious, the eyes full of sadness and power. Air tubes penetrated both sides of his neck, running into his throat, giving him the ability to breathe.

Neither Scott nor Jean recognized the man—if that was indeed what he was—either by face or name. But it was immediately clear to everyone present that—despite his soft voice and genial manner—this was an extremely dangerous entity.

"Well met, vannnnnguard," the soft voice purred. "Is there a prrrroblemmmm?"

"'Problem?'" Marl repeated in a small, frightened voice. "No, no problem."

"No problem that I know of," the chief of guards echoed.

"'Problem' is too strong a word," Marl went on. "Non-problem."

The spy had heard about all he could stand. "What are you people afraid of?" he complained. "You're of mutant caste, are you not? And that's a human—barely," he added, pointing at the floating man.

"Fool," the chief of guards admonished him. "Surely even you have heard of Prior Turrin."

The spy's jaw dropped. "That—thing—is Prior Turrin? B-but according to the holo-grids, he was presumed dead at the raid on Everfields—nearly three years past! H-how is it possible that he is here now?!"

"Me?" Turrin responded. "I attribute it to clean living. Come, child," he said, reaching out with his cannon arm and drawing Nate to him tenderly.

"S-Slym? Redd?" Nate said timidly, unsure of whether to allow himself to be guided any closer to this scary-looking man.

Jean? Scott signaled silently.

He may look horrific, was Jean's telepathic reply, *but I'm sensing genuine concern for Nate. Awe, actually.*

"It's all right, Nate," Scott told the boy out loud. "I think he's a friend of ours."

Nate allowed himself to be guided by the cannon arm into the stranger's lap. The spy looked completely astonished.

"What is with you people?" he demanded of the guards. "The man is a convicted anarchist!"

"Firm!" the chief of the guards agreed. "But he's also de only endurable part of dis whole city." He looked cryptically at the spy, as if daring him to understand what he meant.

"Gennntllemen," Turrin said, turning to the guard troop, "let us examinnne your 'find,' a child, burdened by…prosthetics? And metal?

Not even sssssynthetics...such as...my own? ...Hardly a reason to disttttuurrb...Ch'vayre, I think. Why call attention...to yourselves? Upset the statuuss...quo?"

His tone was gentle, his suggestion friendly, but there was no mistaking the silent threat behind Turrin's words. And the guards understood him, beyond a shadow of a doubt.

"Be a download if'n we got no more Y chromes," the one with the bottle said, scratching his head thoughtfully.

"Turrin has always kept us maxed on the amenities—true," his boss agreed. "If we annoyed Apocalypse for no reason—"

"I can't believe this!" the spy cried out, enraged beyond all control now. "He's black-mailing you! Intimidating you by threatening to cut off your party supplies?"

The chief guard turned to his accuser, as Turrin, with Nate in his lap, made his way toward the gate that led into the city proper, followed by Scott and Jean.

"You don't know what it's like," the chief guard told the spy, "to be posted in this festering pit. Prior Turrin could make it a lot worse if he chose."

The chief turned toward the little procession as it paused by the gate. "Our apologies, Unit Dayspring," he told them. "Welcome to Crestcoast."

"No! I refuse to accept this!" the spy ranted. "I will take this matter directly to Apocalypse himself! For years now, there have been rumors of survivors of the massacre at the Askani Hold—of mutant traitors cloaked in the form of humans! Isn't it clear that this unit—?!"

But the chief was in his face now, forcing the spy back against the wall. "I cannot conceive," he said, "of any reason why anyone would deliberately subject themselves to life within these city walls. Any more than I can picture a less threatening trio than the Unit Dayspring."

He turned and bowed at Scott and Jean, then bowed lower to Turrin. "Prior, a moment," he begged. "What should we do about our powers, now that they've been primed?" He held up his hands, still glowing red from the aborted attack on Scott.

Turrin held up his human hand. "Improvise," he suggested, then turned away, still holding Nate in his cannon arm.

The spy's eyes widened in terror as the guards turned their attention to him one final time. Flames flashed from the glowing hands. Flesh melted and evaporated.

Nathan saw it all, watching over Turrin's shoulder as they retreated into the city with Scott and Jean. It was so horrible, he could hardly bear to look.

"G'journey, traveler," Nate whispered, swallowing hard, "wherever you wind up."

"Thank you for your assistance, Prior Turrin," Scott said as they descended a flight of steps into the streets of Crestcoast. "I must confess, we were not aware there were places where humans such as ourselves lay claim to any power and influence."

"Nothing to speak of," Turrin said modestly. "Much like a cadaver rulinnngg the morgue. Crestcoasst...was once a major city. Now it is a tomb where the walking deaddd... come to die. Yet it serves...a purpose."

"Prior," Jean said, "we forwarded a cargo several weeks ago?"

"'It' arrived unharmed, Redd," Turrin told her. "You will discover...we are quite efficienttttt...in all matters."

"Such as 'disposing' of that fellow traveler?" Scott asked, thinking of the spy's horrible death. "Wasn't that a bit excessive?"

"Not when...you consider what...would have become...of the boy hadddd...he been turned over to Ch'vayre," Turrin pointed out. "We are at war, here...for not only ourrrr... future...but that of the entire planet. Some-timessss...we are called on...to make difficult choices...lest they be made...for us. Or had you not noticed...my friends?"

He gestured around them at the miserable streets, where hordes of people—wretched humans, the robots and androids that were called "synthcons" in this era, and the scum of the mutant caste—lay sprawled in miserable positions, huddling for warmth and comfort.

Turrin shook his head sadly. "This is a dark world in...which we live," he said, "and will remainnnn...so until someone...arrives to lead us to...a better place. Until someone can offf-fer...us hope."

Though the battered and broken, the disil-lusioned and the disenfranchised, the hopeless and forgotten who littered the streets around them could not know it yet...

Hope had now arrived.

Chapter 10

The moon shone down on the decaying city of
Crestcoast. The night was still. The streets were
empty. It was after curfew.

The rooftops, too, were empty—except for
one. It overlooked the back alleys of the run-
down, forsaken Bayside quarter. The soldiers of
Apocalypse, not about to risk their lives in the
narrow, twisting streets, stuck to the main
roads. They did not venture here.

Which was why this particular rooftop had
been chosen. On this fine, moonlit night, Jean
Grey, for the past eight years known as Redd
Dayspring, sat with the child known as Nathan
Dayspring—Nathan Christopher Summers.

Three years had passed since they'd been
rescued by Prior Turrin. Three years of guerrilla
warfare against the regime of En Sabah Nur—
Apocalypse—and the corrupt mutant overlords
who served him.

It was the same moon she'd grown up staring at through the window of Charles Xavier's School for Gifted Youngsters—only older. By two thousand years. Then, she'd been called Jean Grey. As Professor Xavier's first student, she'd been taught how to control her mutant powers of telepathy and telekinesis.

Two hundred decades later, here she was, passing on a similar set of lessons to her young son. But teaching Nate was often difficult.

"Try it again, Nathan," she urged.

"But it's painful," Nate complained. "I can't, Redd, I—"

"Concentrate," she said. "Again."

The boy held out his left arm—the one that had been transformed by the techno-organic virus. For years, it had been nothing but metal cables, coils, and microcircuitry, melded with bone and blood.

"Can't you do it for me?" he begged.

Jean shook her head. "A. I'm not with you twenty-four hours a day, and B. you are fully capable of using your own mind to morph your body."

Nate gritted his teeth as he made another painful effort.

Slowly, the arm began to morph. Skin crept

down from the shoulder toward the elbow, wrapping around it and advancing over the wrist and hand. Metal cables became tendons and muscle fiber, before disappearing beneath the new-grown skin. Moments later, the transformation was complete.

"Here you go," Nate grunted, holding up the arm and wiggling his fingers. "One normal-lookin' Nathan Dayspring. Satisfied?"

"Proud, Nathan," Jean said. "You were born with certain abilities that make you special. Slym and I just want you to fully develop your mutant powers so that—"

"So that what, Redd?" Nate challenged. "So the happy little Dayspring unit can keep passin' for humans? So that I don't embarrass my adoptive parents? So we can keep movin' from city to town and country to city—just to keep one step ahead of Apocalypse's stage doggie, Ch'vayre?"

Nathan's face was flush with rage. All the frustrations he'd been keeping down were suddenly boiling over.

"I'm tired of runnin' and hidin' for no reason, Redd!" he cried out, his voice echoing from the rooftops. "I'm sick of pretendin' to be something I'm not!"

He leaned on the edge of the roof's retaining wall, staring down at the decaying buildings. Tree roots wound in and around the broken doorways, and vines sprouted from the cracks in the walls.

Jean looked down at the boy tenderly. She could feel his pain, sense it telepathically. It hurt her as much as if it were her very own. Nate was like those buildings he stared at, she realized—he, too, was decaying, in need of care and mending.

"Nate," she said softly, "whether someone else calls you a mutant, a human, or a fish, nothing changes what you are inside."

"And what's that, Redd?" he asked, turning to face her, the tears on his cheeks glistening in the moonlight. "What am I on the inside?"

Jean wasn't sure how to answer. How could she tell him he was destined to grow into the man called Cable? How could she explain that he would spend the rest of his life leading a rebellion against Apocalypse and his minions, making one difficult choice after the next, sacrificing his own happiness on behalf of a dream which began in the mind of Charles Xavier—long before Nathan Christopher Summers was ever born?

How could she say those things without revealing that Redd and Slym Dayspring were actually his parents, Jean and Scott Summers?

She didn't dare.

"We've explained this to you before," she said lamely. "So long as Apocalypse is looking for us, it's necessary that we hide among the humans and synthcons. We—"

"Why doesn't *he* hide from *us*?!" Nate demanded hotly. "Why don't we go after him instead?" He stared up at her, a challenge in his eyes. He had forgotten, in his anger, to maintain his control over his body metamorphosis, and his arm and right eye had returned to their diseased appearance.

Jean took the horribly mangled metallic arm in hers. "Someday, we may," she told him. "But for today—"

"Today," he finished bitterly, "I have to pretend I'm not a freak."

Jean sat down on the retaining wall. What could she say that would comfort him? Surely he was not ready to know that they had long ago become members of the Clan Rebellion— guerrilla soldiers under the command of Prior Turrin. No. Nathan needed time to grow, to learn about himself and his abilities, to discover his destiny, untroubled by the pressures of the present.

These training sessions of theirs, she now realized, took more out of the boy than he had ever admitted. The poor kid was exhausted.

"Come here, Nathan," she told him, pulling him gently down next to her. "And listen closely."

"Ye—eah?" he said, yawning and allowing his head to drop onto her shoulder sleepily.

"No matter what happens to you in your life," she began, straining to find the perfect words. She wanted her words to burn their way into his consciousness, and be there for him long after she and Scott were gone.

"No matter what happens to you, the way you look, the choices you make, the times you feel so alone—know that you're not a freak. Always know that there are people who care for you. Who believe in you. Who love you. Today, tomorrow, and yesterday."

Nate did not reply. Had he even heard her, or was he already fast asleep? Jean drew her head back to look at his now-peaceful face. "Did you hear me, Nate?" she asked.

He opened one sleepy eye, and gave her a faint nod before closing the eye again. Then he nestled closer against her, for warmth, for comfort—and in gratitude for her words and the fact that she was there.

How long has it been? Jean asked herself as she cradled his sweet, nine-year-old head in her arms. Eight years since she and Scott had been psionically yanked into this era! Through all the running, the hiding, the deceptions— Jean smiled at the memory of it all, and hugged Nathan harder—despite all the hardships of those eight years, she knew she wouldn't have traded a single moment of it.

Three hundred miles away in the capital of En Sabah Nur's empire, tortured screams echoed through the halls of the Citadel Apocalypse.

And once again, as he had so many times in recent days, the man called Prelate Ch'vayre stood as silent witness to what he believed to be the death of a dynasty.

He stood against the stone wall of the chamber, behind the right shoulder of Apocalypse. Before them Stryfe, now nine years old, tormented a poor, wretched human who had displeased him.

"Enough playing with your toys, Stryfe," Apocalypse told the boy who would one day be emperor. "Share with us the latest manifestation of your growing psionic powers."

"Yes, Father," the boy said obediently. Then, turning to the man, he asked, "Do you want to live, human?"

"Y-yes, L-Lord Stryfe," the man stammered.

"You didn't convince me," Stryfe said, grinning. He pointed his hand at the man's chest and closed his eyes.

A reddish glow shot from Stryfe's outstretched hand, burning a huge hole in the human's chest. The man's face contorted in pain as his insides burned to ashes. Soon, there was nothing left but a small pile of smoking cinders. Stryfe kicked them away and turned triumphantly to Apocalypse.

Ch'vayre stood silently as Apocalypse applauded. He gritted his teeth. Was this what Apocalypse's goal for survival of the fittest had come to? Was pain and suffering and cruelty—the slaughter of innocents for amusement—all that their "master race" of Homo superior had to offer the rest of the world?

"That was fun," Stryfe said, giggling. Then his smile suddenly vanished. "But it didn't even scream first. I hate that."

"Do not downplay your accomplishments,

my son," Apocalypse told him. "Every day, your mutant abilities grow stronger. Soon you will be my equal, as well as heir to the world which is your legacy, Stryfe."

The boy bowed low before Apocalypse, and En Sabah Nur was pleased. "G'morrow, child," he said, dismissing Stryfe. "It is late."

"G'morrow, Father," Stryfe said, turning and leaving the chamber.

"Sire?" Ch'vayre said when the boy was gone.

Apocalypse sighed in annoyance. "What is it, Ch'vayre?" he asked.

"It is about the boy," Ch'vayre said. "Again I feel I must point out, that by your own 'Laws of Natural Selection'—by accelerating the boy's mutant ability as you have, you are not only robbing him of his childhood, but you run the risk of destroying any hope that he might grow to be a—"

"Childhood!?" Apocalypse roared, cutting Ch'vayre off in mid-sentence. "What care I for this boy's 'childhood'?" The disembodied heads focused their angry gaze on Ch'vayre, and he felt himself lifted off his feet and help-lessly slammed back against the stone wall of the chamber.

"Some two thousand years ago," En Sabah Nur went on, "I infected this boy with a techno-organic virus simply because I needed him to survive it—to prove he was worthy to one day serve as a vessel for my ageless power!"

Ch'vayre felt himself being lifted telekinetically into the air. There he hung, suspended near the ceiling, while Apocalypse continued to rant at him.

"His sister, Rachel Summers, and her accursed Clan Askani robbed me of ultimate victory then, stealing him from me. It was good fortune, indeed, that I learned the child had been time-switched to this era. I destroyed the Askani—breaking the long peace—for their arrogance and held him in my arms at last!

"But still, my enemies—the rebels—are everywhere. The battle is not yet over! Do you truly believe I care, for a moment, about the boy's childhood?" Apocalypse boomed. "Concern yourself, Ch'vayre, my Prelate, with stopping those who would rise against me!"

He dropped Ch'vayre to the ground, then glided out of the room, leaving Ch'vayre alone with his injuries and his thoughts.

Once before, long ago, Apocalypse had

mentioned something to him about the techno-organic virus he'd infected Stryfe with. It had shaken Ch'vayre then, but he'd gradually forgotten about it.

But now, the picture rose up before his eyes. "Techno-organic," he repeated aloud. "Like the diseased, ravaged body of the child from the Askani Hold?"

Vividly, he saw the image of the child, snatched from his grasp by the human couple who were not humans after all. They had been there with the Mother Askani. She had called the red-haired woman "Mother."

Stryfe had never exhibited any signs of ever having had a techno-organic virus. But the child at Askani Hold had. *Could it be?* he wondered, more alarmed than he had ever been in his life.

Could it really be?

Chapter 11

They gathered in the back alley, as usual, just before the stroke of midnight. There were about a dozen in their ragtag band, hardened now by years of guerrilla warfare. Turrin nodded to his lieutenant, a scruffy, unshaven man by the name of Skerrit. "Are we ready?" he asked.

"Redd is not here yet," Skerrit replied. "Slym? Do you know where she is?"

"She is with the child." The reply didn't come from Slym, but from a synthcon called Gyak.

"We shall wait for her for another five minutes," Turrin told them. "No longer."

Two minutes later, Redd arrived. She was clearly troubled, judging by the look in her eyes. As she entered the alley, Scott—Slym, that is—was in the middle of objecting to something Turrin had apparently just said.

"All I'm saying, Turrin," he explained, "is that we need a clear idea as to what it is we hope to accomplish on tonight's raid."

"Why is that...Slym?" Turrin asked. "Because you feeel...too much blood...has been lost...of late?"

The wise eyes of the bearded man grew darker, deeper. "Perhapsss...you are right," he admitted. "Perhaps the time hasss come...for someone elsssse...to take up the fight?"

Seeing that Redd had arrived, Turrin turned his attention to her. "Redd," he asked, "you will be joinnning us...of course?"

"Yes, Prior Turrin," she answered. Then, after a quick glance at Scott, she turned back to their leader. "Would you excuse us for just a moment?"

"Of course," Turrin said, indicating that his troop should retreat a short distance down the alleyway, giving Redd and Slym some privacy.

Up for a quick telepathic chat, Scott? Jean asked him. *Husband to wife?*

We really should get going, Jean, he signaled back. *We're on a very tight time tab—*

It's about Nathan.

What's wrong? he wanted to know. *Isn't his condition still in remission? I haven't noticed it getting any worse—*

No, it's nothing physical, Scott, she reassured him. *It's emotional. He's going through a very tough time right now—*

And he needs his father to spend some time with him, instead of running off on one secret raid after another, he finished for her, already struck by the truth of what she'd been about to say.

You'd think, he added, *for someone who spent his entire youth in an orphanage, I'd be a bit more sensitive to someone who's going through the same feelings of confusion and alienation I experienced when I first learned of my optic blasts.*

Scott could have kicked himself for his unforgivable insensitivity. *I'll go to him now,* he said. *I'll explain to—*

Whoa, Scott, Jean signaled. *I didn't tell you this so you can start beating up on yourself. It's been eight years, but we're both stumbling around in the dark here as far as parenting goes. But working together, we'll pull this off.*

Why don't I doubt that? he agreed, taking her in his arms and kissing her face, still unfamiliar after all these years. To Scott Summers, it was always Jean's face he envisioned when kissing Redd. After all, they were still the same people inside.

I'll talk to Nate in the morning, he said, kissing her once more.

In the morning, she agreed, as their lips met yet again.

"Ahem," Turrin's gentle voice rang out. "For a unit unable to...legally bond," he said, "you certainly spend a lot of time in a... perpetual clutch. Time which I suggest could...be better...spent in service to the...rebellion."

Jean grinned at the man she'd come to admire and respect over the last three years. "If that's your way of saying we're on an endless honeymoon, Prior," she replied, "you're right."

"After three years, Turrin," Scott added, "you certainly can't question our dedication to the battle to overthrow Apocalypse."

"Not all of us are as naive as Turrin, Slym," Skerrit said. "I, for one, am curious as to why two tainted humans—such as yourselves—are so interested in the affairs of those of us who are not even allowed the opportunity to give birth to the favored caste, mutants?"

"I'll be more than happy to explain the motivation of the Dayspring unit, Skerrit, in detail—after we return from this evening's raid," Jean told him.

Reminded of the lateness of the hour, the little band of rebels set off toward their target, unaware that they were being watched from above.

Sitting in the branches of an old tree that overlooked the alley, Nathan Dayspring was astonished by what he'd just seen and heard. "I can't believe it!" he whispered out loud. "Redd and Slym—members of the Clan Rebellion!?"

So that was their secret! All during his years growing up, Nate had sensed that Redd and Slym were holding something back from him. Some secret they could not, or would not, share with him. Now, Nate felt sure he'd uncovered the mystery.

How proud he felt of them! And how worried for their safety. No wonder they hadn't told him what was going on. They were afraid he'd worry—or worse—that he'd do what he was doing right now.

Following them.

The little band reached their destination within the hour, sneaking past the searchlights of Apocalypse's fleet of police hovercraft by using a series of forgotten tunnels that wove their way throughout the once-thriving metropolis.

The tunnels shielded them from their enemy, at the same time providing the access they sought to the secret labs of Apocalypse's scientists.

Here, the band of rebels hoped to find a way to free an entire world from Apocalypse's hundred-year reign of oppression.

They emerged from the maze of tunnels and started to disarm the security network protecting the lab. Surprisingly, they met no resistance. The place was deserted, with none of Apocalypse's soldiers nearby.

"Why does it feel like this was much too easy?" Jean wondered aloud.

"It does not surprisssse me, Redd," Turrin said. "Arrogance has lonnng...been a trademark of...our most...despised overrrrlord."

"'Sides," a fighter named Siddard added, "this is hardly a secured area. Sub-sub-sub-sub-basement."

"Siddard is correct, Redd," Gyak, the synth-con, said. He was concentrating hard, attaching his cable ports to the nearest control console.

"This section has long been forgotten,"

Gyak went on. "Classification: low security area."

"To anyone but you, Gyak," one of the others said admiringly. "After all, you're the only synthcon in the world that can use a maintenance console as a back door into the complex's lab-'puters."

"I do indeed possess the abilities necessary to accomplish the task," Gyak responded.

As he said this, Gyak's maneuverings set the console into action. Almost immediately, a holographic projection began to form in the air before them—a green, twisting tower in the shape of a double helix.

"Filos of the high ground!" Skerrit gasped. "What is that?!"

"Classification: bio-centric hologram," Gyak informed him, "showing rendering of disintegrating deoxyribonucleic acid helix, Homo-sapien specific."

"What's that supposed to mean?" Skerrit asked.

"Supposition: a large portion of this laboratory complex is dedicated to the creation and execution of an airborne virus genengineered for the sole purpose of retarding production of human DNA polymerase, which will result in species cessation or extinction."

The rebels stood there, stunned, frozen by the enormity of the discovery. Despite Gyak's complicated terminology, there wasn't one of them there who didn't understand what was meant—a virus was being produced here that could destroy all of humanity!

But to Scott and Jean, it meant something even more specific.

Scott, Jean signaled him. *Do you realize what this is?*

I do, he responded silently. *I recognize it from Professor Xavier's files. It looks exactly like Stryfe's Legacy Virus!*

Above them, crouched on a ledge, Nathan Christopher Summers watched, unseen. He knew that if Redd and Slym found out that he'd followed them here, *his* life functions would be the ones that would be ceasing. But from their horrified expressions, it looked to Nate as if they'd just seen a ghost!

"Gyak," Jean asked, "how far are they from turning this theoretical disease into a reality?"

The synthcon did some instant calculations. His skeletal head swiveled on its metal spine. "I do not have enough information at this time to make an estimate, Redd," Gyak told her. "It is clear, however, that there is only one thing stopping them from releasing the virus. So far, the virus cannot tell the difference between human and mutant DNA. Unleashing the virus as it is now would mean the end of all life on the planet Ear—"

A reddish light flashed, blinding them all for a moment, as the terrific boom of an explosion hit Gyak full force, blowing him apart.

"Not *all* life, synthcon!" a voice rang out—a voice that chilled Scott's blood.

"01 10 11001100 10 10—" Gyak's mouth moved, but all that emerged were number sequences, as his brain fried in the heat of the blast.

"Gyak!?" Siddard gasped. Then he, like the others, looked upward, toward the source of the explosion. There stood Ch'vayre, at the head of a troop of Apocalypse's soldiers, all firing bolts of red energy at the tiny band of rebels.

"As it has been ordained since the beginning of time," Ch'vayre said, gazing down at them triumphantly, "the strong will survive!"

Chapter 12

Siddard could not believe his eyes. "Ch'vayre?!" he gasped. "We've been set—"

Before he could finish what he had to say, Siddard was leveled by a powerful blast from the weapons of the attackers.

But Ch'vayre finished his sentence for him. "Set up?" he guessed. "Yes, flatscans, indeed, you have been set up. You've grown overconfident after so many months of 'victories.'"

Red laser light flashed, electrical energy crackled, and two more of the rebel band were blown to smithereens. The others returned fire as best they could, while scrambling for cover in the bowels of the laboratory complex.

Above the fray, alone in an alcove that overlooked the scene of the battle, Nate looked down on both rebels and ambushers. He could barely contain his anger and alarm.

"This is too rabid!" he muttered to himself.

"They need my—" He tried to leap down to the next level, where a catwalk would have led him to a ladder. But Nate found that he could not move even a muscle.

"My? Wha—? I can't move!" he gasped, struggling to break free of the bewildering spell that held him frozen in place.

And then he heard it. The voice in his head. He'd heard it once or twice before in the last few years—the voice of consolation, of patience, of sage advice. The lady's voice.

Nathan, stay, it told him now.

Nate felt the blood rush to his head, the fight-or-flight response as the adrenaline coursed through his system from the shock of hearing the voice. But for the moment, he could neither fight nor flee. The voice commanded, and he had no choice but to obey.

Down below, the battle raged on. One of the attackers had the advantage over Skerrit, flying at him and kicking him squarely in the jaw. Skerrit reeled backward.

"Redd!" he called out in desperation.

"I've got him, Skerrit!" Jean called out as she leapt at the attacker, her sword slashing so fast that it was nothing more than a blur.

The attacker went down, groaning. "There,"

Jean said. She stood over the fallen mutant, but didn't deal the fatal blow. "That will show him we can be as generous as his master."

Skerrit shook his head angrily as he got up, massaging his injured jaw. "Again, you merely wound one of them? Just once I'd like to see you kill one of these mutated aberrations!"

Jean shook her head. "The day we stop showing compassion for our enemy, Skerrit," she said, "is the day we *become* the enemy."

It was true enough. But Jean couldn't help wondering what Skerrit would think if he knew that both she and Scott were mutants themselves...

Farther down the corridor, one of the attackers, a nine-year-old, attacked another rebel. His dagger pierced its victim again and again, so quickly that it was practically invisible. Stryfe had killed the man already, but he didn't stop. He intended, as always, to wring every drop of enjoyment from his blood sport.

"What fools these mortals be," he muttered, unknowingly quoting Shakespeare, the immortal bard of twenty-five hundred years ago.

Two rebels were dead before they'd even registered the boy's presence. Having finally finished with his victim, Stryfe turned to the other members of the ambush squad.

Ignoring Ch'vayre, who was busy fighting Prior Turrin farther down the corridor, Stryfe took the liberty of giving orders to Ch'vayre's soldiers without the Prelate's knowledge— orders Ch'vayre certainly wouldn't have approved of, had he been able to hear them.

"Now, good men," Stryfe shouted to the troops, "despite Ch'vayre's orders to take these people alive, I'd like this to be over quickly. And the remains of the rebels sent to my father, Lord En Sabah Nur—he who is the Apocalypse—one extremity at a time."

"Fall back!" Prior Turrin shouted to the remains of his guerrilla band, as he remained locked in battle with Prelate Paladin Ch'vayre. "I will seek to put sommmme...debris...between us and...our attackkkers."

With his blaster-hand, he shot at the walls and ceiling of the tunnel. Chunks of metal and masonry broke loose and fell onto the attacking soldiers, forcing them to fall back.

"Skerrit! Redd! Set the explosives!" Scott shouted. "If nothing else is accomplished tonight, we're going to destroy this complex!"

Scott saw that one of the attackers had leveled a blaster in his direction. Forgetting that his friends in the guerrilla band knew nothing of his mutant powers, he leveled an optic blast at his assailant.

The attacker flew backward into the wall and dropped to the ground, unconscious. But Scott's mutant powers had not gone unnoticed. Skerrit was staring at him.

"Wha—?" he gasped. "Slym, you're one of them? A mutant? I don't get it!"

"Now isn't the time to discuss it, friend," Scott told him, firing another optic blast to keep the attackers off balance while Jean laid the explosives. "Suffice it to say that not every mutant subscribes to Apocalypse's racism."

The explosives laid, the rebels retreated down the tunnel. As they backed away, Turrin and Scott fired at the walls and ceiling, causing rubble to fall and making it impossible for Ch'vayre and his men to pursue them.

Turrin, observing Scott's powers, shook his bearded head in admiration.

"It's called an 'optic blast,' Turrin," Scott informed him, letting loose yet another as Jean flew up to the ceiling, to lay more explosives. Turrin's curious gaze followed her upward, as did Skerrit's astonished one.

"We never told you about our powers," Scott said to Turrin, "because we believed you were safer if you didn't know the truth!"

"And what is that ttttruth, exactly?" Turrin demanded, raising his eyebrows.

Scott returned Turrin's gaze. "That we have a common enemy," he answered cryptically. "Even if it is for entirely different reasons."

On the other side of the wall of debris, Ch'vayre scowled angrily. "They thought they were clever, barricading themselves farther into the complex!" he muttered. But in so doing, he also realized they had blocked their own way out.

"Order the torch cannons from above," he told his second-in-command, "before they cause any more damage."

"Right away, sir," the soldier said.

Ch'vayre turned to Stryfe, who had come up behind him. Gesturing toward the destroyed corridor, he said, "This, child, is the reason one does not go about killing at random. Had you not slaughtered their comrades so savagely, we might have managed to corral them before they panicked!"

Stryfe looked down at the ground, seemingly abashed. "Forgive my boyish enthusi-asm, good Ch'vayre," he said.

But Ch'vayre could hear the mockery in the boy's voice. Stryfe knew very well that he was Apocalypse's favorite—no matter what he did, it would be fine with his father, En Sabah Nur. Ch'vayre wished that he could teach the boy some sense. But such an act would mean death at the hands of his Master.

The soldier Jean had wounded lay on the ground at Stryfe's feet. Now, seeing the young-ster staring down at him with a strange, fasci-nated, almost hungry look in his eyes, the wounded man squirmed uncomfortably.

"Lord S-Stryfe," he stammered, gasping in pain, "what are you looking at?"

"I was just thinking," Stryfe replied thoughtfully, stroking his chin. "Once you're already wounded, why not die anyway?"

As Stryfe toyed with him, the wounded man's screams resounded throughout the tunnels. Even Nate heard them in the alcove far above. Nate now stood before one of the maintenance consoles that were a back entrance into the complex's computer network.

The voice of a woman had led him here,

allowed him to walk only in this direction. And now, it was as if she stood over his shoulder, guiding his hands as he worked the controls of the unfamiliar machine. The screams of the dying soldier below reached Nate's ears, but not his consciousness. His attention was riveted by what his hands were doing, unbidden by his brain.

Ignore the screams below you, Nate, the voice instructed him now. *Concentrate on the console before you.*

"But I don't understand the first thing about 'puters," Nate protested weakly. *Relax,* the voice told him. *Open your mind to me. I will tell you all you need to know.*

"You have to brainside me to do it?" Nate asked, annoyed at being manipulated this way.

My apologies, little brother, the voice said. *I have no time to be subtle.*

"Yeah. Well once ya get the chance, ya have a lot of explaining ta do!"

Nate's voice trailed off as a hologram took shape in the air before his astonished eyes. "Wow!" he exclaimed, amazed at what his hands had done. "A holographic overview of the whole complex. This is so—!"

Shush, child, the voice of the lady interrupted him. *There is still more you must do...*

Down below, Stryfe looked up from the sight of the grisly, smoking remains of the soldier he'd just finished playing with. There, far above the site of the battle, he noticed an eerie light coming from an alcove set into the walls.

Looks like somebody is somewhere they shouldn't be, he thought.

"Ch'vayre," he called out, "you'll excuse me a moment?"

"With all due haste, M'Lord," Ch'vayre said, eager to have the horrible child out of his sight once more.

"As for the rest of you," Ch'vayre said, turning to his troops. "What is keeping those torch cannons? Even with the complex surrounded, there is always the chance they might escape, let alone the damage—"

But his words were cut off by a sudden blast that blew a hole in the wall of debris in front of them. And out of the hole stepped the man with the flaming eyes.

"Trust me, Ch'vayre," the man said. "If escape was our goal, we'd have been long gone!"

"Wha—?" Ch'vayre gasped in disbelief.

"They are taking the fight to us!"

As the man with the flaming eyes approached him, followed by the red-headed woman who flew above him, Ch'vayre suddenly realized where he had seen them both before.

"You!" he cried in astonishment. "The man and woman from the Askani Hold."

"'Redd' and 'Slym,' please," the woman corrected him. At the same moment, the man shot another blast at Ch'vayre from his amazing eyes. Ch'vayre ducked, just in time.

But his men were retreating, heading for cover. Ch'vayre knew that he, too, had to retreat, at least for the moment.

His mind was racing madly as he ran. So! He and his soldiers had suffered a temporary setback, but that was nothing. Soon, they would once again, inevitably, reverse the tide. And when they did—when they captured this insanely courageous rebel band—they would gain control of not only the legendary Prior Turrin, but the mysterious man and woman from Askani Hold as well. The ones who had escaped with the child.

Scott and Jean pursued the retreating soldiers.

That's it, Jean, he signaled. *Keep Ch'vayre angry and off balance until the others finish their work of laying the rest of the explosives.*

Will do, Scott, Jean replied, *but if we die here and now—before we get to see our son and daughter again—I'm going to be fairly angry myself!*

Up in the alcove, Nathan worked away furiously at the computer console. The voice had stopped speaking now, but the force behind it was still manipulating his hands.

When the tap on his shoulder came, Nate at first thought it must be the woman, trying to get his attention. But then he realized—the woman only spoke inside him!

Wheeling around, Nate found himself staring into the face of a boy who looked exactly like himself—or, exactly as he would have looked, if he didn't have the awful disease.

"Excuse me?" the boy said to Nate. His hand on Nate's shoulder tightened into a fist, grabbing his shirt. "I know everyone who serves my father—and you're not one of them!"

Chapter 13

Nate stared at the boy. *This must be Apocalypse's offspring!* he thought. *The odds of me surviving this—*

"Just dropped considerably?" the boy suggested aloud. "True."

Nate's jaw dropped, and his eyes widened in astonishment. "You just read my mind!" he gasped. "It was like you were thinking the same thoughts as me! How is that—"

"Possible?" Stryfe shrieked, his face contorting in white-hot fury. "It isn't—it's not possible! There is only one Stryfe—only one heir to the throne of Apocalypse! There is only one Chaos Bringer!"

Stryfe looked as if he might explode with anger at any moment. Nate lifted his diseased left arm to shield his face.

"Truth, Stryfe?" Nate offered meekly. "Being the Chaos Bringer was never one of my life goals."

Uncanny, he thought. *If not for the longer hair and my own diseased body…*

"There is a certain similarity between us, no?" Stryfe suggested, again finishing Nate's thought for him. "I cannot bear to be anything less than unique, Nate."

So saying, Stryfe raised his perfect left arm and pointed it at his diseased twin. Orange flame lashed forth from the fingers and engulfed Nate, at the same time lifting him into the air, where he hung suspended, shrieking in agony.

"Odd," Stryfe commented calmly, "I can almost feel the pain I am inflicting on you."

Nate heard Stryfe's voice through his torment, as the flames licked about him, not consuming him, but inflicting horrendous torture.

And then, there was that other voice—the woman's voice—speaking to him in urgent tones that Stryfe could not hear the way he heard Nate's unspoken thoughts.

Concentrate, Nathan, the voice commanded. *Allow all the power that is yours to command, little brother, to flow through you. Pure. Uncontrolled. Unbidden.*

"Wha—?" Nate did not understand what

the voice meant, but he tried to do as it was telling him. And, just as with the 'puter, the power seemed to come naturally to him.

He felt the golden energy coursing through him, mingling with the flames that surrounded him. The orange fires flared outward suddenly, knocking Stryfe off his feet and sending him reeling backward, screaming in the pain of his own making, now sent back at him, double-force.

Look upon this and know, the voice said, *there is much more to the psionic abilities you possess than even those who know you best might suspect.*

Stryfe lay unconscious, though still breathing, on the floor of the alcove. And now, suddenly, Nate began to feel something very strange happening to his body. His left arm, already mostly techno-organic, began to sprout new cables and microcircuitry, growing six, eight, ten feet outward from his body.

At the same time, the skin of his right arm popped open, and new cables sprouted outward from underneath. His face began to melt away, as wires and microcircuits grew everywhere on his body.

"Wha—what is happening to meeee?!" he shrieked in terror, falling to the floor.

Do not fear what you are, the mysterious, inner voice answered him. *What you became when you were infected by the trans-mode virus. Given time, your powers will develop naturally, your body and mind will be as one, and you will have no peer throughout the universe! Until that day comes, relax and know that I am here for you...*

The voice faded away. And slowly, as the sounds of battle raged below, the cables and microcircuits began disappearing, or at least, retreating back beneath the skin, which seemed to heal itself as quickly as it had disintegrated.

Nate felt weak, disoriented, shocked beyond all measure by what had just happened, by the revelations the voice had made, and most of all, by what he had done to Stryfe, who still lay prone on the ground before him.

He forced himself to turn his attention back to the 'puter terminal. There was still work to be done. And from the sound of things down below, there was very little time to do it.

Ch'vayre stared at the battle going on around him. "The rebels have caused enough trouble this day!" he told his second-in-command.

"Find Lord Stryfe and fall back—I want this complex leveled within the hour."

"But what about the research—the virus?" his subordinate asked.

Ch'vayre's frown deepened. "That will be my responsibility," he said.

One thing was still bothering him. Turning to the two rebels who stood fighting together on his left, he called, "You two are clearly mutants! By the lips of Apocalypse! Why would you dare oppose him?"

"It's a freedom thing," the red-headed woman replied as she zapped one of Ch'vayre's soldiers. "You wouldn't understand."

Scott leveled an optic blast at another soldier who was about to vaporize Jean with his energy weapon. *Jean,* he said telepathically, *this isn't like it was with the X-Men. We can't afford the risk of losing our lives in battle—we have Nate to worry about! One of us—as in you— has to leave now before it's too late.*

Scott, Jean signaled back, *I just got the signal from Turrin.*

Are we ready to bolt?

Sooner than later. He says we have two minutes to get clear!

At that very moment, Ch'vayre's attention

was distracted by the arrival of his second-in-command, who flew back into the chamber, holding Stryfe in his arms. The boy was limp, his face white as death.

"Stryfe!" Ch'vayre shouted. "Mathus—what happened to the boy? Is he—?"

"Alas, no," Mathus replied, clearly wishing it were otherwise. "Wounded somehow. He'll recover soon."

"Bring him here," Ch'vayre ordered. "I will take him directly back to the Citadel. See that none of the rebels leaves here alive!"

Ch'vayre realized this went against his original orders. So did his plan to level the complex. But things had changed since they arrived to ambush the small band of rebels. It disturbed him that Turrin's troops included mutants, and that among them were the man and woman from Askani Hold. He didn't know what it meant, but he suspected that the child held the key—the child he'd given them in exchange for the Mother Askani.

He hadn't wound up capturing her, either. Ch'vayre sensed, more strongly than ever, that he'd made a terrible mistake all those years ago—a mistake which might now mean the end of Apocalypse's empire.

Meanwhile, as Ch'vayre flew off with Stryfe in his arms, the rebels began their retreat, having laid explosives throughout the tunnel. Ch'vayre's men, who were under orders to blow the complex up, had no idea that their opponents had the same intention and had already set the timers ticking.

The rebels flew upward, out of the grasp of the soldiers, and huddled on the hovercraft that was Prior Turrin's lower half. Jean flew alongside them, on her own power, not afraid to show her mutant abilities now that they all knew the truth about her and Scott.

Scott—that boy with Ch'vayre? she signaled.

He must be the clone, Scott said, echoing Jean's thoughts. *The one Rachel told us about all those years ago, during the assault on Askani Hold. But we—*

"'Tention Redd!" Jean and Scott froze at the unexpected sound of Nate's voice, calling to them from the alcove just to their left.

"Nate!" Jean gasped. "What are you doing here?"

Nate ignored the question. "If you're leaving anyway," he said, "can I grab a ride?"

Jean hugged him fiercely yet tenderly, as the rebels quickly evacuated the complex. And not a moment too soon, either. They soared skyward just as the explosion ripped the roof off the laboratory building.

It was a tremendous explosion, vaporizing the entire complex—and with it, all the soldiers who were still inside.

Turrin stared at the fires, at the hurtling pieces of metal, and nodded slowly. "We have accomplished much this day...my fffriends," he said. "Though in the...futurre, we might want...to calculate a wider margin for error."

Skerrit was scratching his head. "I want to know," he said, "how the 'plex blew that high. That was quite an explosion. Much more than the explosives we set."

"That was me," Nate said sheepishly.

"What did you do, Nate?" Jean asked him.

"As near as I can tell," he replied, "I progged the 'puters to self-destruct the place—top to bottom."

They came to a soft landing on a rooftop overlooking the alleyway where they'd first gathered that night. Scott and Jean hugged Nate, feeling his arms and back for any signs of injury, just to make sure he was all right.

"At this point," Skerrit said, shaking his head in admiration, "nothing you Daysprings do surprises me!"

Scott smiled at his son. "Aside from the fact you shouldn't even have been here," he said, "how was it possible for you to do what you did, Nate? Humans have been banned from high-end technology for years. I don't think you've ever touched a computer before today."

Nate sighed. "You're gonna think I'm crazy," he said, "but I had help. She told me how to do it."

"She?" Jean repeated.

"The woman in my head," Nate said. "The voice I hear sometimes. Her name is—Rachel."

While the streets of Crestcoast were filled with the muted sounds of celebration, the man once known as Scott Summers stole a moment away in a quiet, secret place.

The subterranean room was dark, except for an eerie light that played on the table in the middle of the otherwise bare chamber. On that table lay the body of an old woman. Tubes ran from her neck, her nose, and her eyes to a machine above her—a machine which sustained her life functions, keeping her comatose condition stable.

Until tonight, Scott had believed that that

was all the machine had been able to do. But now, he knew better.

"For the past eight years," he told his daughter, Rachel, "Jean and I have assumed you were in an irreversible coma—totally shut off from the outside world. I should've known you'd never accept that."

He bent close over her, stroking the white hair on her head tenderly. "Thank you," he whispered. "Not only for what you did today, but for bringing us here in the first place. For bringing us all together—as a family. Thank you, and I'm sorry. Sorry I never treated you much like a daughter when I had the chance. I just wanted you to know how very proud I am to have been your father."

He swallowed hard, blinking back tears. "In case I never made it clear to you before," he whispered, "I love you, Rachel Summers."

At that very moment, standing outside the gates of Apocalypse's Citadel and staring out into the starry night, Ch'vayre was coming to a realization of an entirely different sort.

His heart had been troubled for a long time. But tonight it had all become clear.

He could no longer pretend not to see what

his eyes had witnessed, nor ignore that which his heart knew to be true. His entire life, he had shared the same goals as the Master he served—En Sabah Nur. He had made himself believe what Apocalypse had always professed: the true strength of *Homo superior*—the reason for their vaunted position in the world—lay in the compassion and understanding they had for all life forms, not just mutants like themselves.

But seeing Stryfe in action tonight, it was clear to Ch'vayre that Apocalypse had come to believe that strength meant domination, not compassion. Whatever humanity was left in the boy's soul was fast disappearing. Soon, he would be the perfect empty vessel to hold all that was dark and vile about their "Master."

While Ch'vayre accepted the fact that it was too late to save the boy that Stryfe might have been—it was not too late to save the countless millions of innocents of every race who would suffer and die if the boy lived to become the Chaos Bringer.

Chapter 14

Two more years had passed. And with them, times had once again changed.

The rebellion went on. More successful strikes were launched against laboratories working on the Legacy Virus. Sooner or later, it looked like Prior Turrin's rebels would succeed, at least in a limited way.

Ah, but time was quickly running out. For every day, Stryfe grew stronger in his evil mutant powers. Soon, he and Apocalypse would become one, forever.

And time was also running out for Nathan Christopher Dayspring.

It wasn't supposed to end this way. When Jean and Scott had been psionically yanked into the future, they had welcomed the opportunity to raise the son they had lost.

All the happiness and rewards, the sorrow and the sacrifices—their lives together, as a family in the here and now—were about to end this day.

They watched, hovering over the horrific, yet pathetic, figure of their son as he lay on his deathbed, looked after by the dwarf healer, the most skilled practitioner available to Prior Turrin's troops. The healer turned from their comatose son and looked at Prior Turrin, shaking his head.

"Redd...Slym..." Turrin said, sighing deeply, "I'm sorrrry. There's nothing more we can do for him."

Jean felt a lump rising in her throat, and tears stinging her eyes. She could hardly bear to look at Nathan—or, more accurately, the thing that had once been Nathan.

For now, it was nothing more than a tangle of wires, cables, microcircuits, bolts, and other techno-organic matter, with bits of skin here and there, and blank, white eyes. The mouth was open in a perpetual, silent scream of agony. Tubes fed into the metal veins from an apparatus hanging over Nate—an apparatus which seemed at least as human as Nate himself. Jean turned away, unable to look anymore. But Scott continued to stare, his face grim, his hands clasping Nate's between them.

Turrin hovered over the group, shaking his head sadly. He himself had been transformed into something other than human many years ago. But his wounds had been the results of battles, not a virus. And he had been an adult in his prime, not an innocent child of eleven.

"I'm sorry," he repeated. "Even without Healer Prxuse's...prognosis, it isss...clear the boy's...condition iss...terminal."

"But how could this have happened, Turrin?" Jean protested helplessly. "The techno-organic virus in Nate's body has been in remission for years! Why, even a month ago, there was no sign of its progression!"

"As you havvve said..." Turrin agreed. "But the boy's bodddy...has been changing as well...in recent months. I believe the ancient term...was 'puberty.'"

"You're saying the maturation of his mutant ability...is somehow agitating the virus?" Jean asked.

"But one of mannny theories, Redd," Turrin replied. "As sound as anyyy other. The truttth is, even after all these years...we don't know enough...about the boy, the disease, or your entire Dayspring unit...to draw...any definitivve concluuusions. While we've always respected...your privacy...I must point out that your secrets...may have cost Nathan Dayspring his life."

Scott turned toward Turrin, his face angry. "Don't talk about him like he's dead, Turrin," he said in a hoarse voice. "I haven't given up hope. He hasn't given up fighting, and none of us are going to give up trying to save him."

The dwarf healer applauded, grinning hideously. "'At's the spirit, Slym!" he cried in a thin, high-pitched voice.

Scott turned to him. "You sound optimistic, healer," he said hopefully.

"Optimistic? No, I wouldn't say that, Dayspring," the healer replied. He lifted his magnifying glasses onto his forehead and looked up.

"Since y'allowed me to gene read him," he said, "it's been one surprise after the next. Foremost, what we always assumed was bionics? Actually, the metal is alive."

He reached out, fingering the cables of Nate's forearm. "See?" he asked. "Warm to the touch—blood felt coursing through 'veins.' Distended? Yes. Ugly as all things? Yes. Beyond help? Yes. Surprised he's lived this long. Might want to consider 'alternatives' to this quasi-life. End his suffering, no?"

The healer blinked, waiting for a reply from Scott.

He got one. "That's not an option, Doctor," Scott told him, in no uncertain terms.

Jean stepped forward urgently. "I have to believe there's another way!" she said. "For the past three years, I've been tutoring him on the use of his biokinetic abilities—if I could only reach him telepathically through this coma, through the psi-interference, we could help him save himself."

"And iffff you cannot, Redd?" Turrin asked. "What then? Are you prepared to sentence young Nathan…to a life even more horrific than my own?" He drew a long breath through the tubes that provided him with oxygen. "Wouldn't the embracccce of death…be more mercifulll?"

At Apocalypse's Citadel, much the same dilemma—death as an alternative to pain and suffering—faced Prelate Ch'vayre. Once the undisputed ruler of Apocalypse's elite cadre, he was now experiencing something akin to a crisis of faith.

He stood watching—marveling, really—as

before him, Apocalypse, the ancient shriveled man inside the huge blue armor with its disembodied, smiling heads, worked his magic on the boy, Stryfe.

The youngster hung suspended in midair, in the middle of a vertical pillar of yellow flame, screaming in agony, over and over and over again. The disembodied heads looked on, smiling.

"Please, Master, I beg you!" Ch'vayre shouted over the roaring of the flames, over the screams of the helpless boy. "If, for no other reason than to preserve the sanctity of your own immortal soul—you *must* abandon this madness!"

Apocalypse did not turn toward his Prelate, who stood, helpless, in the grip of four enormous guards.

"You mistake madness for destiny, Ch'vayre," he said simply. "Today brings about the culmination of nearly four thousand years of personal evolution. Born into slavery, I—who was once called simply En Sabah Nur—have spent hundreds of lifetimes ignoring the ravages of time, defying the demands of nature, forging myself into the master of all manner of man and mutant! All of which would have been meaningless—had I not found the child called Stryfe!"

As he said the name, another, even louder scream burst from the mouth of the boy. Ch'vayre winced and tried to break free. But the guards, who were even larger than him, held firm.

"I named him after an ancient enemy of mine," Apocalypse told his Prelate. "A man whose own machinations nearly destroyed me—but who, in the end, only made me stronger. But just as I ultimately triumphed over all who have dared oppose me over the eons—so, too, am I prepared to use the young boy as the final vessel for my near infinite power!

"So cease your pathetic pleading on his behalf, Ch'vayre," Apocalypse concluded. "The moment you took him from Askani Hold, you delivered him to this fate. You delivered him unto me."

Ch'vayre lowered his gaze to the ground, sure that he was about to be dragged off to his death. But, to his surprise, Apocalypse was apparently not finished with him quite yet.

"I must confess," Apocalypse said, still not turning around, "that I fail to see the problem you have with all of this. For as long as I have spoken, I have preached the survival of the fittest! That often necessitates a lesser life force being sacrificed for a stronger one."

Ch'vayre raised his head once more. "But for the sake of light and darkness, Lord," he said passionately, "he's just a child."

"Less than that, actually," Apocalypse corrected him. "He's a means to an end."

Apocalypse raised his right hand, and at the signal, the four guards dragged Ch'vayre backward toward the entrance to the grand chamber.

"You have served me well over the years, Ch'vayre," Apocalypse called after him. "Do not force me to have you killed on the eve of my greatest and final victory."

As Ch'vayre stood in the entryway, watching in horrified fascination, Apocalypse turned his full attention back to the task at hand.

"Soon, boy," he said to the tortured child who hung suspended in the pillar of fire before him, "soon, the voice that has been muted by pain—the eyes blinded by your transubstantiation—will speak and see the words and worlds as they exist—in my image!"

Chapter 15

At last, it had stopped. The pain which was all Nathan Dayspring had known over the past three days was suddenly replaced by an overwhelming state of—nothingness?

No, not quite nothingness. He could see, through a grayish-white haze, the room before him. As if from a great distance, he could see the rest of his unit—Slym, Redd, along with Turrin and others—hovering over him, with pained, worried looks on their faces. He could hear their words chipping faintly against his consciousness.

Despite the realization that he was alone— trapped somewhere on the knife's edge between life and death—the first-born son of Scott Summers refused to go quietly into the night.

Redd—Slym…! he tried to psi-signal them, *don't leave me now, when I need you most!*

He envisioned himself whole again, as he used to be. He was reaching out toward them, his face panicked. *Please d-don't abandon me— like my parents did.*

I'm afraid they can't hear you, little brother...

The voice! The voice in his head—perhaps he wasn't as alone as he had thought.

Turning in his mind, he saw himself facing a pretty, sober-faced girl in her teens, with shoulder-length red hair, and large, penetrating blue eyes. She wore a tunic, leggings, and gray boots. The two of them stood in a limbo-like space, with nothing else in sight.

Nate stared at her in wonderment. *You...?* he gasped. *Y-you must be Rachel! The voice in my head all these years?*

In the ectoplasm, as it were, the girl said. *This is my favorite version of myself, you know—Rachel Summers at age fourteen. Before Charles Xavier was assassinated—before Ahab and his hounds— before the power of the Phoenix.*

I don't have any idea what you're talking about, Nate said. *But—why did you call me 'brother'?*

Sorry, Nate, Rachel told him. *I guess I am kind of skimming over a lot, but then, we don't have much time.*

She walked toward him, her eyes locked urgently on his, and put her hands tenderly on his shoulders. *The reason I called you my brother is more than half the reason I'm here,* she said. *I want to let you know that you have a much larger support system—a larger family—than you ever imagined.*

Does this mean, Rachel—you came to take me home? he asked.

Her answer was a warm embrace. Then, with a fierce, final squeeze, she let him go. *Just the opposite, really, kiddo,* she told him sadly, stroking his hair. *I'm here to explain why you'll never have a home.*

Turrin had left the room. Jean and Scott lingered over the prone figure of their son for a long time before either spoke.

Finally, after a deep sigh, Jean said, "Slym—Scott, I hate to do this, but we have to get going. Tonight is the culmination of three years of raids—putting together the pieces of this virus Apocalypse's scientists have been developing. The same virus we believe will be unleashed in our time as the Legacy Virus." Putting a hand on his arm, she added, "Bottom line, Love—it's now or never."

Scott didn't turn to face her. Still staring at the comatose figure of his son, he said, in a choked voice, "I can't. He needed me once, and I let him go."

He stroked the small, limp hand which he held in both of his own. "Even if there is nothing I can do—other than be here for him," he whispered, "I won't—I can't—leave him alone again. I'm sorry, Jean. You'll have to do this without me."

"Never without you, Scott," Jean replied, embracing him. "You're always with me in my heart."

She kissed him warmly, tenderly, passionately.

"I love you, Jean Summers," Scott whispered when their lips parted.

"As if I didn't know that already?" she quipped, her mouth curling into a brief, wry smile.

"Take care of him, 'Slym,'" she said, heading for the doorway. "Tell him I'll be here in the morning, tell him I'll sing his favorite song. Tell him—I love him."

"In the morning," Scott repeated, nodding in agreement. He looked sadly at the woman he loved so much, knowing it might be the last time he ever saw her alive. "G'journey, 'Redd,'" he said.

And then, she was gone.

The eerie light from young Stryfe's transfiguration filled the night sky with shades of a coming apocalypse. The people in the teeming city below looked up in awe and fear. They didn't know that a new phase in the long, long life of the man once called En Sabah Nur was dawning. But still, they felt the dark power emanating from the place, and they avoided the shadow of the towering Citadel that was home to their genetic overlord.

But deep within Apocalypse Hold, two key members of the Clan Rebellion suddenly materialized to take a final, perhaps fatal, stand against Apocalypse's century-long reign of terror.

They found themselves in a corridor, empty to all appearances, lit only by a yellow glow coming from its distant end. But as they approached it, the glow grew steadily brighter, until it was blinding.

Jean slowed her pace, and Turrin, hovering above her, slowed as well. The leader of the Clan Rebellion looked down at the woman he knew as Redd Dayspring and was troubled by what he saw in her eyes.

"Redd, what issss wrong?" he asked her. "You ssseem apprehensive..."

"Turrin—that light!" she told him, wincing in its glare. "It is almost purely psionic in nature. The interference is preventing me from scanning ahead. It means we could be walking blindly into—"

All of a sudden, there was a popping, fizzling series of noises, and Turrin's lower, metallic half began short-circuiting. Horrified, Jean watched as flames burst from the circuits controlling the tubes that fed him oxygen. They roared around Turrin's head. His eyes went dead white with shock and pain. And then— the flames started shooting out from his head itself!

"Turrin!" Jean shouted. "Are you all right?! It's a psi-attack of the highest order. The synapses in your brain are exploding!"

Concentrating as hard as she could, Jean put her own psi-powers to work. "Hold on!" she told him. "Given time, old friend, I'll be able to reverse the—"

"No...time," Turrin gasped, reeling backward and sinking to the ground. "Go...on..."

Jean backed away, emotionally torn. She wanted to stay and help her friend, but reason told her he was right. The mission had to be accomplished, even if it cost the life of their leader.

Yet Jean stood frozen, unable to tear herself away. And then, she heard a voice from behind her. A voice she'd known, and feared, ever since she and Scott had arrived in this time.

"Your friend will live."

Jean wheeled around and saw the enormous figure, silhouetted against the glare of the psionic light. "Ch'vayre?" she gasped. "You did this?"

He came toward her, and as he did, she backed away and ran over to Turrin's side. She knelt before him, shielding him from any further attack by Ch'vayre.

"I apologize for the cruelty," Ch'vayre said, surprising her. "But I refuse to allow 'others' to be involved with what we must do."

Jean was confused. What was he talking about? Why wasn't he attacking? Why hadn't he killed Turrin with his first psionic blow?

"'We,' Ch'vayre?" she repeated. "What are 'we' going to do?"

"We're going to attempt that which has

never been done," he told her, straightening up to his full, enormous height. "We're going to stop Apocalypse."

Nathan Dayspring was staring across the grayish-white void at the strangest thing he had ever seen—a metallic skeleton, not quite complete, with only a right eye and only part of a right arm and leg. Yet, although it stood facing him, in mirror image, he felt somehow akin to it.

There is your home, Nate, Rachel said, pointing to it.

Wha—? But even in that instant, Nate understood what it was he was staring at. *The techno-organic part of my body?! That's what I looked like on the inside before the virus started growing again!*

He looked at Rachel, and she nodded her confirmation.

B-but why are we—why am I separated? he asked, beginning to feel the panic rising inside him.

Just then, he heard Slym's alarmed voice, distant yet close by. Turning, Nate saw him, distorted and huge, looming over the limbo-like space. He was holding Nate's hand, yet

Nate stood apart from him. Looking down at his right hand, Nate saw that flames were shooting from it!

"Healer? What's happening?!" Slym was shouting.

"Convulsions!" came the healer's voice. "Losing vital signs."

Nate stared at Slym's gigantic, misshapen image, at his own flaming hand that Slym was holding. *Wha? Slym?*

They're worried about you, Nate, out there in the real world, Rachel told him. *There's not much time. To be brutally honest, kiddo, all your suffering is happening because you're not trying hard enough.*

Hard enough to do what? Nate demanded. *If my body is at war with myself, what can I do?*

Rachel held her hands out toward him, palms upward. *Here and now, Nate,* she said, *you possess as much, if not more, power than me or any other telepath combined. Telepathically, you are strong enough to sense a stray thought a continent away. Telekinetically, you could extinguish a star with something less than a conscious effort.*

You've got a few alpha waves on order, girl, Nate protested, shaking his head in disbelief. *That's just crazy.*

No, Nate—it's your heritage, she insisted. *It's the reason Apocalypse wanted you in the first place. And although you won't remember any of this when—if—you survive, it's important you know it here, in your heart.*

She began walking slowly toward him, closer and closer. Then, incredibly, she walked right through him so that their heads occupied the same space.

As the Mother Askani, I brought you to this time, she told him. *I even created a clone to serve as a decoy—in the event Apocalypse struck before you could be trained in the use of your powers. When I realized I was too weak to help you, I sent for our parents from the past. For ten years now, your mother has tried to educate you about your abilities—training you'll need, little brother, to telekinetically hold the techno-organic incursion back from completely enveloping you.*

Suddenly, she began to fade from view, although her voice continued to echo inside his head.

An entire world is counting on you, she said, as he looked down at his own body and the techno-organic skeleton standing next to it. *It will mean sacrificing your other abilities, literally fighting on a cellular level every day of your life, making sure you live to see the next dawn. But to answer your question: Yes, you can do it. You're a Summers. You can do anything.*

The voice faded, then disappeared. Nate stood there, frozen, awed by all she had told him. And as he watched in astonishment, the techno-organic skeleton moved slowly toward him—as Rachel had—until it slowly, painlessly, entered his body, merging once again with his human flesh.

As the memories of what Rachel had told him began to fade from his consciousness, the distant voice of the healer, growing closer now, drowned out what had come before.

"Lost him—sorry."

"Noooo!" Nate screamed, straining with all his might to break out of his limbo-like state. "I'm not dead! I will not give up!"

"Dayspring, please—he's gone," the healer said gently, as Slym bent over the lifeless figure of his son. "Allow him to—"

"No!" Scott shouted, the tears stinging his eyes. "I'm his father. I would know if he were gone! So long as there's a spark of life within him, I won't leave him. I will not give up!"

Suddenly, he noticed his son's body move

beneath him. Then, Nathan raised his head upward, pulling himself out of his coma.

"Yyyouu're...ssstilll...hheerre?" his voice cried out. Quickly flesh began covering the metal that had invaded his body. "You didn't....leave me...?"

"Nate?" Scott gasped as he embraced his son. "No, Nate, I didn't leave you."

Scott hugged his living, breathing son. It was incredible. A miracle—no, more than a miracle! Nate was pulling his body together, the way Jean had taught him! His mutant power must have somehow grown stronger than the virus.

Nathan suddenly broke free from the embrace. "Have to...go...," he said, still trying to catch his breath from the enormous effort he'd just made. "We're needed—"

"You don't need to do anything but get better," Scott told him, holding the boy tenderly in his arms. "Now relax, and—"

"You don't understand, Slym," Nathan said. "It's Redd—somehow, I know! It's like our minds are...one. I can sense her thoughts. She's in trouble...alone."

He looked urgently into his father's eyes. "She...needs us."

Chapter 16

The psionic fire in the great hall of the Citadel lit up the sky for hundreds of miles around. Apocalypse stood facing Stryfe. The boy hung suspended in midair. His body was scorched yet not consumed by the yellow pillar of flame.

Stryfe's arms were raised, his mouth wide open in a silent scream, his eyes open yet seeing nothing. But it was from this boy that Apocalypse would soon draw eternal, all-powerful life.

Apocalypse stared hungrily at the boy. Within the imposing blue armor, the body of the old man that was the present vessel for his existence had grown withered beyond recognition. The flesh began to shrink away from the bone, revealing the hideous, evil skull beneath.

"At last!" Apocalypse cried out in triumph

as he moved toward the boy. "The vessel is prepared to receive my true essence, allowing me to make manifest my eons-long dreams. I will be strong—I will endure."

Stryfe turned his eyes toward the voice. His mouth opened wider, in sheer agony.

"Try to see past your pain, child," Apocalypse told him. "Take comfort in knowing that your sacrifice will usher in the final age of mutantkind!"

The disembodied heads that hovered in the air above the armor disappeared. And as the old man unhooked himself from the harnesses which held the armor to him, his thoughts turned inward to a hated face from the past...

"Tell me, Xavier," Apocalypse muttered aloud, his skeletal face breaking out into a hideous grin, "can you see me from the mud and mire that is your grave? Do you see that I was right all along? That I outlived you, Magneto, Sinister, and Holocaust—even your descendants, the Askani! I outlived you all!"

He stepped out from the shelter of the armor and floated through the air toward Stryfe. They would merge now, and eternal life would be his—what need would he then have for armor?

Taking the boy in his arms, he shouted in triumph, "I stand where all the others have fallen! Just as I predicted—I have survived!"

"So far, Apocalypse—so far!"

As the voice rang out, Apocalypse felt himself jolted, as if by an enormous bolt of electricity. "ARRRGH!" he grunted in pain. "A psi-attack!"

"I am sorry, My Lord—truly."

It was Ch'vayre's voice! Apocalypse couldn't believe it—but looking up, he saw that it was true! Ch'vayre stood on the balcony above the great chamber, staring down at Apocalypse. In one hand, he held the limp body of one of the guards who had been assigned to protect the chamber while the transfiguration was in progress.

And by Ch'vayre's side was a woman with red hair. Where did he know her from?

"Step away from the boy, Apocalypse!" the woman called down to him. "No matter how much contempt you hold for any life other than your own, no matter the amount of blood you've caused him to spill through your sick and twisted manipulations of his body and soul—Stryfe is a living, breathing individual with a right to his own life!"

"You presumptuous insects!" Apocalypse screamed, stretching out his bony hand toward them and sending a thunderous bolt of psionic fire their way. "I have lived and planned and prepared for this moment ALL MY LIFE! Residing in one body after the next, I did everything and anything it took to ensure not only my continued existence, but the growth and dominance of all Homo superior! One life lost, or one hundred thousand—what possible difference does it make as long as we survive?!"

Another bolt blasted the balcony. Stone fragments flew in all directions.

"Not that you will be able to answer me, woman," Apocalypse raged on, "for I can promise you, we will be on opposite sides of the grave forever!"

Another bolt flashed out and the balcony's roof collapsed onto itself, burying everything underneath. Apocalypse waited until the smoke and dust cleared, and there was only silence left. Then he turned his attention back to Stryfe.

"Now come to me, boy," he said hungrily. "I have waited four thousand years for this moment. Come, know the kiss of Apocalypse.

Know the gift that is eternal—Noooo!"

He pushed the child away from him in blind, white-hot rage. "No! Th-this cannot be! This is not a mutant! Not a true life-form. It is a gene-copy—a clone?"

His hand reached out for Stryfe once more. And once more, Apocalypse's touch revealed the truth. "Yes! He possesses the ability, but not the capacity to maintain my essence!"

His mind made an instant mental calculation, trying to overcome this sudden, critical reversal of fortune. "In my true form, I am weak," he realized, "yet I should still be able to enter his body until I can find a suitable vessel."

He tried to will the merger to happen—but it didn't work. He remained trapped in the withering, creaking body of the old man!

"Somehow, he is resisting me!" Apocalypse realized, beginning to panic. "For more centuries than I can remember I have flowed from one body to the other. Never has anyone been able to resist the process!"

"Maybe, Apocalypse," a new, male voice rang out, "because no one has had help resisting you before!"

In a flash—both dreadful and wondrous—

the creature called Apocalypse saw beyond the earthly bodies, and recognized the essences of those who now stood against him. Scott and Jean Summers, and Nathan Summers—the boy who would become Cable.

Had he met them before this moment, he would have been able to figure out their identities. Now it was too late. They leapt down at him from the shattered balcony, and the reality of what had happened dawned on Apocalypse.

"Curse the Mother Askani!" he screamed. "Only she could have brought the three of you together to stand against me! Only she could have left this—this THING in the place of the child I sought—the one I needed! But I will not be bested by defenders of a dream long dead! A dream I myself killed!"

Bolt after bolt of psi-fire leapt from his fingers at them. In response, they acted as a family. For the first and perhaps the only time in their lives, they struck as one.

For a long time, the battle was a standoff. Optic blasts and telekinetic strength ranged themselves against the timeless power of Apocalypse, who, though greatly weakened and outnumbered, was still a formidable foe.

And then, in mid-battle, Scott felt it. Suddenly—inexplicably—he felt the psionic tug at the base of his skull. Scott Summers had felt that tug only once before—when he and his wife were yanked across time to this era to raise their son and battle Apocalypse. With both those tasks now so painfully near completion, it appeared suddenly to Scott that their time here was over.

But it had come too soon! The battle was not yet over. And there was another reason—with a pang in his heart, Scott Summers realized that he wasn't sure he wanted to go home.

Jean, he psi-signaled, *how much longer do we have?*

It's impossible to say, Scott, she replied. *Something has been anchoring us in this era—a power greater than mine, certainly. With that power gone, it could be a matter of hours—or moments.*

The force had actually tugged them backward, so that they now stood beyond the grand archway, outside the great hall. Nathan ran back to see what had happened to them.

Apocalypse, blinded by the pillar of fire in which he floated along with Stryfe, could no longer see them. "Where did you go, children?" he called out. "Did it suddenly occur to you that I possess all the power I need to defeat you? That I will endure as I have always done?"

Scott and Jean looked at each other.

Scott, she signaled him, *if what he says is true...*

He wouldn't need Stryfe! he finished for her. Seeing that Ch'vayre had managed to extricate himself from the stone rubble which had buried him up on the balcony, and had now come down to fight alongside them, Scott turned his attention to his son.

Nate?! While Ch'vayre is distracting Apocalypse—I need you to reach out and disrupt the psi-bond between the boy and his 'father'! Block whatever telepathic energy you feel!

Whatever ya say, Slym! Nathan signaled back. Stepping inside the pillar of fire, he came up behind Stryfe and took the unconscious boy's head in his hands.

"No—" Stryfe moaned weakly. "I...am...the...Apocalypse...I...I am...his...soul son."

Nate nodded slowly. "Let's see what we can do about changing that," he said.

In moments, the pillar of fire surrounding the two boys had extinguished itself. It sucked itself upward toward the high, domed ceiling, dragging Apocalypse along with it. Bolts of lightning flared from En Sabah Nur's fingers, and his scream rent the night.

Seeing their ancient enemy writhe in agony brought no joy to his attackers, however. They knew that by blocking the telepathic exchange between Apocalypse and his heir, they were ending a ritual that had endured for eons.

And in the Apocalypse host's final cry, Scott and Jean Summers felt only emptiness.

The pillar of fire disappeared. The old man's body fell to the ground, smashing itself against the flagstones. Dust flew, and when it cleared, nothing remained but a pile of bones, the eye sockets of the skull wide and empty, the mouth open and screaming.

Scott and Jean looked down at it, holding hands, well aware of the weight of the moment.

"I—I can't believe it's over," Scott said. "The pain. The suffering. The sorrow. All of it. Over."

"Scott," Jean said gently, "it had to be done. You know that, don't you?"

And then, the tug came again. And this

time, there was no mistaking it. Looking at each other, they could see their bodies fading into invisibility. Their time here was over.

Nathan looked up and saw what was happening. His eyes widened in alarm. "Redd!" he cried. "What's happening to you?! You and Slym are leavin', ain't ya? Don't!"

Jean reached out her arms for him. "Oh, sweetie," she said, "we don't want to. But we can't stop it! Oh, baby—let me hold you one last time—"

But it was not to be. Nathan rushed for her—and ran right through her!

"Nathan?" she gasped.

Sorry, Jean. He can't hear you. It was Rachel's voice. No mistaking it. Jean could still see Nathan. Scott, still not quite faded, was helping his son up from the floor where he'd fallen to the ground. Behind them, Ch'vayre held the limp body of Stryfe in his arms, as he sat on Apocalypse's empty throne.

Turning, Jean saw, to her amazement, a red-haired teenager standing in front of her. *Rachel.*

We're on an altogether different plane of existence now, she told her mother. *You're on your way home—Scott is about to join you. And me...well, I'm on my way to who knows where.*

Rachel! Jean cried out. *What Nathan told us before—is true! You've been with him all these years, haven't you? From the moment you fell into your coma—you've been watching over him.*

Watching over my brother...and my parents, yes, Rachel replied. *What else are big sisters for, right?*

Rachel! This can't be happening! I—

Five minutes ago, Rachel interrupted her, *my physical body finally died, Jean. The long wait is over.*

Suddenly Jean's eyes were overflowing with tears, and sobs choked her. Seeing her mother in such pain, Rachel came toward her and placed her hands on Jean's shoulders.

Don't waste a single tear on me, Jean, she told her. *I've lived more than my share of life—fought more than my share of battles. Remind me to tell you about the fifty years I spent forging the Clan Askani some time. Until then, I'd like to ask one last favor.*

Name it, Jean said, wiping away her tears.

You and Dad—all of us—accomplished a lot here. Apocalypse had practically destroyed our family, but we managed to take it back from him. We rose from the ashes. Again.

I won't be here for the rest of the fight, Mom. So I was wondering if you'd take back the one thing I took from you. I'd like you to carry it with you, and think of me. I know there's a lot of pain and hurt attached to the name Phoenix—but there's a lot of good, I hope, as well. I tried to do the right thing for all of us. I tried to save us all. Please, Jean—will you?

Jean Grey looked into her daughter's eyes. The Phoenix Force had taken hold of both of them for a time, and given them great power. It had done much good, and then, its darker side had done great evil, too. But without it, there would have been no Rachel Summers. There would have been no today—and maybe, no tomorrow either.

I—I'd consider it an honor, Jean said, hugging her daughter with a fierce, desperate love. They had never truly been able to be a mother and daughter together—and now, they never would. It was almost too much for Jean to bear. *Rachel—*

I—I know, Mom, Rachel replied, choking up as both of them faded to nothingness. *I love you, too.*

Chapter 17

Scott Summers faced his son, knowing that his time was short. Already, his body had half faded away. Jean had disappeared altogether. He had only moments left with Nate. What could he say to him, to help heal the hurt—to help him carry on after they were gone?

"N-Nate," he said, "there's so much I want to say to you. So many things I want to teach you. I wish I could explain to you why Redd and I have to go—but all I know is that we have no choice."

"Please," Nathan begged, the tears rolling down his cheeks. "Don't leave me, Slym."

He reached out to try to touch Scott's hand, but his own fingers slipped right through, touching only empty air. "I can take the disease," Nathan went on, "I can take down another dozen Apocalypses, but please, I can't do it alone!"

"You'll never be alone, son," Scott assured him. "Not in your heart. Not in the only way it matters—because I'll be there, Nate. Because I love you, son. Remember that, always!"

He held out his hand so that his fingers brushed Nate's. They couldn't feel each other's skin, but they could sense the bond between them.

"You'll be many things to many people," Scott told the boy. "Sometimes, you'll be loved and respected. Other times, you'll be hated and feared. Almost always, you'll be misunderstood. Someday, Nate, you'll be a *cable* that unites the past with the present and the future—yesterday with today and tomorrow. You'll be all those things, Nathan Christopher, but know that you'll never be alone. Never."

The hand was gone. The ghostly figure had disappeared. Nathan Christopher Dayspring shivered with a cold that came from within. Perhaps Slym was right. Perhaps he would never be alone. But one thing was certain— never again in his life would he feel as alone as he did at that very moment.

And then, he heard Ch'vayre's voice calling his name. Turning, he saw the huge warrior, cradling the limp figure of Stryfe in his arms as he sat on Apocalypse's throne. Through all the good-byes, he had sat there, watching, listening. And only now, when the others had gone forever, did he see fit to speak.

"You understand, of course," he told Nathan, "that it doesn't end here. I am but one of En Sabah Nur's followers—one of the disenchanted. But those who are loyal to him—those in positions of power—count themselves in the thousands. There will be many who will search endlessly for his heir." He looked down at Stryfe, whose chest rose and fell as he slept, exhausted but alive. Then he raised his eyes once more to Nathan.

"And they will search, too, for the young boy responsible for inflicting such harm on the Dynasty of Apocalypse," Ch'vayre continued. "I have resources at my command—I believe I can protect both myself and this child. But you, stripling, I fear—"

"I'm not the one you should be worryin' about, Ch'vayre," Nathan brushed him off, feeling a mighty river of strength suddenly coursing through his soul. "From everythin' Redd and Slym told me, Apocalypse went a long way to takin' apart a dream."

He looked Ch'vayre right in the eye. "I'm

gonna put it back together again," he promised. "This isn't the end, Ch'vayre. It's only the beginning."

Jean opened her eyes to find herself lying on the beach, surrounded by a small crowd.

"She's awake!" someone called out. "Thank goodness!"

"Scott...where...?" she groaned. Turning to her side, she saw him lying next to her. Now, as she watched, he, too, began to stir.

"They're coming to, Doctor!" one of the onlookers said. A woman broke through the crowd and knelt at Jean's side.

"How are you feelin'?" she asked Jean in a lilting Caribbean accent.

"Okay, I guess," Jean said, blinking in the glare of the setting sun.

"We thought we were goin' to lose the bot' of you dere for awhile," the doctor told her, helping Jean to a sitting position, then doing the same for Scott. "You bot' been out more dan two hours since you was fished outa da water."

"Two hours?" Jean gasped. "But—we've been gone ten years! How could only two hours have gone by?"

The doctor chuckled, and got to her feet. "We're bringin' an ambulance by, to take you to the hospital an' have you checked out, just to make sure you're okay. Don' move, I'll be right back. Come on, everyone, give dem a little space. Dey need air to breathe, mon!"

She shooed away the curious onlookers, giving the couple enough privacy to get their bearings.

Jean turned to Scott and helped him to his feet. They embraced passionately.

Oh, Scott! Jean signaled. *It's you! We're back!*

Yes, Jean, he replied, nodding. *After all these years, we're back! And obviously, the telepathic rapport we share is working fine, 'Redd,' even after everything we've been through.*

Been through—? Slym—Scott, our trip to the future—helping to raise Nate—saving him from Apocalypse— We're home, back in our own bodies! But what about Nathan Christopher?

W-we accomplished what we were sent there for, Jean—we raised my son—but, I guess it was all we were allowed to do. I guess it was time to come back where we belong.

The doctor said we'd been unconscious on the beach for two hours, Jean told him.

Two hours?! But we spent ten years—!

Don't you see, Scott? It was Rachel! She sent us back—almost to the very minute the Askani took us.

They heard the wail of the ambulance coming down the hill toward the shore. Then they saw it pulling up where the road met the beach. The crowd gathered around it as the paramedics started unloading stretchers.

"Scott—" Jean suddenly said. "I'm picking up a psi-signal. It's from Professor Xavier!"

"What's he saying?" Scott asked.

"Shhh—!" She shut her eyes, straining to hear over the din of the sirens. Then she opened them and shook her head in annoyance. "I lost the signal. But the part I got doesn't sound good. Apparently, there's some trouble at Muir Island. The professor wants us to get over there right away!"

Scott frowned. "Something must be really wrong for him to call us on our honeymoon."

"And they say marriage changes your life forever," Jean said with a smile.

Scott sighed, and returned her grin. "Well, we never wanted normal lives, did we, Jean?"

"No. But it still would be nice, wouldn't it?" she asked, looking up at the mountains and out at the turquoise sea. "We spent the last ten years of our time raising a child, being a family, trying to be like regular people—but it wasn't an even remotely normal existence."

"I know, Redd," Scott said. "But we do what we've always done. We move forward. You with me?"

They both looked over at the ambulance, then at the sheltering line of trees, with a path leading through it.

"Always, Mr. Summers," Jean said, taking his hand.

"Let's go then, Mrs. Summers," he said, leading her down the path.

Behind them as they went, they heard the shouts of surprise from the paramedics, shocked to find their patients had disappeared.

Scott and Jean were at the road now. They found their rental car and headed off, away from the beach. Soon they would be flying toward Muir Island, and another adventure.

"Scott," Jean said, leaning her head on his shoulder as they drove, "do you think we'll ever get a real honeymoon, at least?"

"Redd," he replied, drawing her to him, "when we're together, our whole life's a honeymoon!"

SABRETOOTH
UNLEASHED

He's turbo-charged and ready for action...

"Don't strain, Sabretooth," came a voice from the other side of the room. "You'll pop your stitches. Doctor Mabuse has been working around the clock for the last week, giving you a full system upgrade. You can now consider yourself to be Turbo-Sabretooth."

"You made me stronger?" Sabretooth grunted.

"Yes. We also installed a control device next to your aorta," the voice went on.

"Who are ya?" Creed demanded.

A robotic figure approached the operating table. From what Creed could tell, the figure was actually a man inside a huge green suit of armor. He wore a helmet that prevented Creed from seeing his face.

"I am the Tribune," the man said. "And I have had all of this done to you so you will be able to carry out a very special assassination."

And coming soon...
Gambit: Unfinished Business
Upstarts Uprising